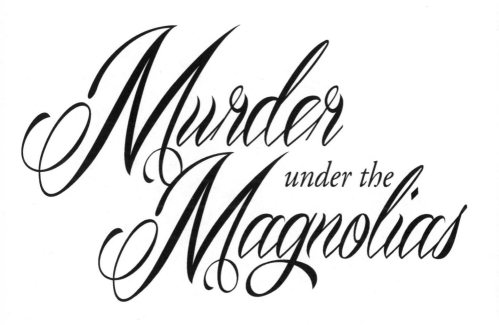

Murder under the Magnolias

CHARMAIN Z. BRACKETT

DIAMOND KEY PRESS

Published April 2016

1

"Grace, we don't have enough roses."

Emmie stepped back from the large floral display she was working on to point out the gaps.

"I thought I ordered enough."

"Well, you did until Jimmy Hughes got drunk last night and came home with lipstick stains on his collar again. He wiped us out this morning."

The thought of Jimmy brought a smile to my face. Jimmy was one of my best customers. God bless him. I don't know what I'd do without him.

"I told her not to give him all those flowers," interjected Beth as she worked on another large arrangement for one of Saturday's weddings.

"Did you call Green's?"

"Yes, but who knew that late March was going to be prime wedding season this year?" Emmie continued. "Apparently, we aren't the only ones with a calendar full of weddings this weekend. They only have two dozen red ones they can spare. They're delivering them along with today's regular shipment. We needed a few more lilies, and the Wilson wedding calls for lots of calla lilies. But I don't think that's enough. I need some pink roses too. There's a 'welcome baby' arrangement that was called in about 20 minutes ago."

"It's always busy in the spring. They're all getting married before

1

the tournament and the annual exodus. It's the perfect time for a honeymoon especially if you don't have tournament badges. How many did Jimmy order, anyway?"

Emmie wrinkled her nose.

"He actually came in this morning while you were out and wanted everything he saw in the cases. Then he asked for more. I saw the ones you had set aside for the arrangements so I didn't mess with those, but -"

That was several dozen roses. I started to panic at first, but then I remembered stashing several in a case we didn't use often just for this reason.

"Yikes. He came in the store instead of calling? Sounds like his fight with Peggy was a doozy this time. Don't worry about it. I think I have this covered."

I walked into the back storeroom, hoping that Emmie had forgotten about this one particular refrigerator. I deliberately put a few boxes in front of it. Out of sight, out of mind. When Emmie got overwhelmed, it was easy for her to get distracted. I knew it was about time for another one of Jimmy's binges. He tended to go on his monthly drinking sprees about the same time each month, and why Peggy Hughes stayed with him, I never knew. I wasn't complaining. I was thankful she did. After I moved the boxes, I opened the fridge, and there were several dozen pink and white roses plus some lilies and even a few irises that he hadn't snatched up as his penance for his wife.

"Emmie, is this enough?"

"You're a lifesaver," said Emmie."These are plenty for tonight's wedding, and we should be okay for tomorrow's two weddings as well."

"Crisis averted?"

"I don't know why I didn't think to look back there."

"I'm glad you didn't or these would be in Peggy Hughes' sunroom about now, and we'd be out of luck. I know Jimmy likes the biggest bouquet he can find, but I planned accordingly. He wiped me out one time too many, and I'll never let that happen again."

Emmie laughed.

"You always seem to be a step ahead of us."

"I'm the boss. I get paid the big bucks to think ahead."

I tried not to laugh as I said that.

"This is perfect. I need to head to the church and get things in place for tonight's ceremony."

"What about the weddings tomorrow?"

"Beth is working on those. I helped her some earlier, but they are small weddings so there's not as much to do."

"Do you need anything else?"

"No, Danny's driving the van, and he'll help me unload things. I can finish this centerpiece that is going on the altar there now that I have enough flowers."

"What were you saying about a 'welcome baby' arrangement that just got called in?"

"Oh yeah. There's one for the Andrews' baby."

The Andrews' baby. I glanced at the floor. I really didn't want to make that. Baby arrangements were already hard enough, but that one would be much harder. I took a deep breath.

"I can do that one really fast if you want," Emmie replied.

No, she had too much else to do.

"It's okay. I can get it."

"Are you sure, honey?"

I nodded.

"Of course." I tried to sound like it didn't bother me, but Emmie knew better. "I can make a baby arrangement with my eyes closed. Just throw some pink and white blooms into a cutesy container with no problem, right?"

I tried to pass it off as if it was no big deal. I noticed Emmie giving me the eye. I knew she didn't believe me. She was swamped so she had to let go of this one.

I've always loved flowers. After a few years of working for another florist, who sold her shop and moved to Myrtle Beach, I decided to take a leap of faith and open my own small floral and gift shop, Grace's Gifts. There's nothing like seeing the expression of joy on the faces of those receiving the flowers. Even at funerals, I'd seen people look at the arrangements and smile.

But it definitely was a leap of faith. It wasn't easy to keep the doors open at times. I was thankful for customers like Jimmy Hughes. Part of me hoped he'd never go to any 12-step programs.

I grabbed a bunch of pink carnations and some small pink and white roses for this particular arrangement. I took a deep breath. Dana and Bill Andrews were friends of mine. At least, Dana was. I wasn't crazy about her husband. She and I were close friends growing up because our grandmothers and our mothers were best friends, and we spent a lot of time together. Things had gotten complicated as adults, and at times, I thought it was probably all my fault.

All Dana ever wanted to do when she grew up was be a mom. They'd tried for years to have a baby. She'd lost several, and doctors gave up hope. Dana and Bill even tried to adopt a baby about 18 months ago. They'd already brought her home from the hospital when the mother changed her mind. It was heart-wrenching to watch Dana go through that. I hated it for her. I felt so helpless at the time because I couldn't do anything for her. It wasn't long after that that things started falling apart between the two of us, or maybe they'd already been falling apart and I didn't realize it. I noticed she started distancing herself from me. She didn't return calls or texts for several months until she found out she was pregnant. I couldn't stop thinking about all of it and started to cry. This just brought up painful memories I couldn't deal with. It wouldn't take long to get the stems into place if I could stop my hands from shaking.

"Why don't you let me finish that one for you?" I heard Emmie's voice behind me. "You can work on one of those wedding arrangements."

I nodded and traded places with her. I followed the pattern Emmie had started and mindlessly filled in the blanks trying to bury my emotions. I was about to finish cutting a few more stems when a pair of hands covered my eyes. There was only one person who did anything like that.

"It's never a good idea to cover the eyes of a woman holding a pair of shears."

I turned to see my husband, and the smile on his face erased any reason I'd had for tears. A mid-afternoon visit to my shop and that grin I hadn't seen in many months could only mean one thing.

"You got it?"

I threw my arms around his neck, and he pulled me close for a bear hug.

"Are you going to let me answer?" he asked.

"You already did. I can tell from the look on your face. I haven't seen you smile in months."

His jaw tightened as I said that last part. He glanced away for a moment. He tried to hide his aggravation, but I knew it was there. Once again, I seemed to say the wrong thing at the wrong time. He'd been working for this promotion for a long time so obviously he was excited about it now, but he hadn't been happy in months.

"Well, if you must know, Mrs. Ward, you are looking at Augusta-Richmond County Sheriff's Department's newest homicide investigator."

"I'm so proud of you, Drew. You've been waiting for this all of your life."

"And tonight, we're going to celebrate. I have reservations for us at Mick's."

"Isn't that a little expensive?"

Again, the look.

"I've been putting a few bucks back from each paycheck for the past couple of months because I knew this was going to be happening. I wanted tonight to be special. I've denied myself steak for months now. I'm getting the biggest one on the menu. I know that my mom will want to have a big party, but this is going to be just you and me."

I smiled.

"Drew, I am so happy for you. You just don't know."

"I think I do," he smiled. "I couldn't have done it without you cheering me on."

"I don't know about that. I haven't been such a great cheerleader the past couple of months."

"You've always believed in me, Grace, even though it's been tough the past few months. The fact that you've stuck with me says more than enough."

Drew had been my hero from the moment I laid eyes on him when I was about 8. He and my brother, Zack, started playing recreation league football together when they were 13. They went to the same school and were in the same classes, but they were never on the same team until that particular year. After practice, he'd come over to our house. I'll never forget those sparkling blue eyes. I guess 8 years-old is a little young to be spying out a potential husband, but I knew I had to have him even then. He still had those deep blue eyes, but the sparkle hadn't been there in a while. Life and the job had done that to him, but for a moment I saw it once again. I hoped it would stay.

"What have you got going on?" he asked as he released me and motioned to my work-in-progress.

"A wedding, but this is Emmie's design so I hope I'm not messing it up."

"Why are you doing Emmie's?"

I looked around, but Emmie had gone. I tried to smile.

"Hope Lily Andrews was finally born."

He nodded, and his eyes wandered to the flowers. I knew he wasn't interested in them, but what else could he say? We'd said it all, or at least, he'd said all he was going to say. And that's where part of our problem was.

"I've got to get back to fill some paperwork out," Drew filled the silence. "Our reservations are for 6. That's the only time I could get. You will be finished by then, won't you?"

"I close at 6, Drew. You know that."

6

"Why don't you let me close?" Beth asked as she walked into the room. Her timing was impeccable, but I knew that was only because she'd been listening at the door. Emmie followed at her heels.

"That sounds like a great idea," Drew said.

He gave me a peck on the cheek.

"Thanks, Beth. See you later, Emmie."

"No problem."

Beth tilted her head and looked at me.

"Are you okay?" she asked.

I nodded.

"You are such a bad liar," Beth said, giving me a quick hug. "Emmie or I can drive Dana's arrangement over there for you too if you'd like."

"I'd appreciate that."

"I'm excited for Drew. I know this is something that he's been working toward for a long time," said Beth.

"This is what he's wanted all his life. He's never talked about anything else except becoming a detective with the sheriff's department. He's worked long and hard."

"Then why such a sad face?"

I gave her the best fake smile I could muster with teeth and all. I knew better than to even look Emmie's direction. I knew she didn't believe me. Beth patted my arm.

"Everything else will come together too," she whispered.

"I hope you're right."

"You need to have a date with your husband. When's the last time you two spent any time together?" she asked.

I shook my head. I couldn't remember.

"You've really been pushing the shop, and we're going to be so busy in the next couple of months with all the weddings you've got lined up for us. Doing that big bridal event in the fall was a great idea. Besides with you gone, I can be in charge."

Beth winked at me although I wasn't quite sure if she was actually joking or not.

I took a deep breath and finished Emmie's design. I knew she'd go back and redo anything she didn't like anyway.

While it wasn't the fanciest restaurant in town, Mick's did have the best steak and seafood. Those were the two foods Drew loved the most. Going to Mick's was a luxury, but it held such special memories. It was the spot where he proposed, and we'd gone for an anniversary or two. I wasn't sure what to wear. It wasn't the type of restaurant that required a coat and tie, but my mother always taught me special occasions and celebrations demanded appropriate attire. That meant no blue jeans or yoga pants or even work clothes. I left the shop in Beth and Emmie's hands and decided to buy a dress for the evening. If he was splurging, I could splurge too. Well, a little bit. I wasn't one who believed in retail therapy. I watched every penny like a hawk. I couldn't remember the last time I'd been to a shop other than my own, except for maybe the grocery store.

It was spring in Augusta. I'm thoroughly convinced there's a place in Heaven that looks just like my hometown does as it comes into the full glory of spring. Of course, Heaven wouldn't have the yellow haze of pollen that leaves many to sneeze, wheeze, and become otherwise uncomfortable. With its multicolored azaleas, sweet-scented purple wisteria, and lovely pink and white dogwoods, Augusta is enchanted and ethereal. It truly lives up to its nickname of The Garden City. I think the azaleas have always been my favorite especially the fuchsia colored ones. And with a week to go before one of the premiere events in pro golf took place in my city, the azaleas were almost in full bloom. Everything had awakened from its winter slumber seemingly overnight, and the trees, grass, and shrubs seemed to know they had to be the exact same color as those beautiful fairways off Augusta's Washington Road.

I hoped I could find a dress. I hated to shop because I was always trying to lose another 10 pounds to be perfect, but that never really happened. They always seemed to linger. It didn't help that there was this fantastic cupcake shop right around the corner from me. Oh well. This past winter was hard. Winter was never my favorite season anyway. It didn't snow here, but the stark branches of the trees and the short hours of sunlight always depressed me. I needed to wear as much color as those spring blooms I saw.

I guess it was my lucky day. I found a knee-length dress in a vivid pink in the first store I visited. I always thought that color looked best on me with my light brown, curly hair. Even if it didn't, I really didn't care because it was my favorite color. And it was on sale. How could you beat that?

I still had time to take a hot bath before Drew would be home. I hadn't relaxed in the tub in what seemed like months. I was standing in front of the bathroom mirror putting on my makeup when Drew came home.

"Has anyone told you today how beautiful you are?" he asked as he stood behind me, slipped his arms around my waist, and kissed me.

"No one but you."

"Good. Maybe we should stay here tonight instead," he grinned before kissing my neck. 'But I promised you a night out to celebrate so I'm going to take a quick shower."

I turned around to look at him.

"Tonight is about celebrating your promotion."

He touched my face.

"Grace, I - " he paused. "I want tonight to be special."

"And it will be."

"I love you."

"I know."

"So tonight -" he started to say something then paused. "Could we just try?"

I nodded.

"I love you, Drew."

He gave me a weak smile.

"I know."

2

As usual for a Friday night, Mick's was packed. I was glad Drew had made reservations. Even so, we had to park almost in the far corner of the parking lot. As we walked toward the restaurant's front door, I noticed a couple. They were standing next to a sports car. I'd never been a good judge of age, but he looked like he was in his 50s. He had dark hair with patches of gray at his temples. He was wearing a suit and tie. He had a crooked nose, like it had been broken, and there was a slight scar along his cheekbone. The woman was considerably younger with long blonde hair. She was wearing a sleeveless red dress. She was beautiful, but something didn't seem right. It didn't have anything to do with the age difference. I wasn't sure what it was. They made an odd pair. They seemed to be arguing about something from the expressions on their faces, but I couldn't hear what they were saying.

Drew spoke to them as we got closer. At first, I thought he was being friendly, but he was a detective so maybe it was something else.

"How's your evening?" Drew asked them.

The man was holding the woman's wrist. She had the most beautiful tattoo. It was odd that I was drawn to it. I don't have any tattoos; I can't do needles. If other people like them, that's up to them. I usually didn't focus on someone's tattoos, but hers grabbed my attention. It was a beautiful butterfly on her forearm, but it was unlike any tattoo I'd ever seen. I think the bright pink color is what grabbed me. It looked like there might have been writing under it as well. I glanced up at her face. She seemed afraid, and then I realized why this seemed off to me. It was a strange sense of deja vu. I got that a lot. The night before I'd had a dream, and this was the woman in it. It was vague, but I knew she was in danger. Her eyes pierced through me in the dream. I didn't do anything to help her then.

"What's it to you?" the man growled at Drew in a thick New York accent, throwing the woman's wrist away from him. She pulled her arms into her chest, covering the tattoo. She noticed my staring. Her eyes seemed to plead with me for a second before she glanced at the pavement.

"Just being hospitable," said Drew.

"Southern hospitality is overrated."

"Being polite never goes out of style," Drew lowered his voice. That was Drew's police officer voice - low, deliberate, and authoritarian. Something about this whole situation bothered him, and it bothered me as well. The man glared at Drew, and I watched as my husband slightly pulled his sports jacket back to reveal the badge and gun he wore on his belt. Instantly, the man's demeanor changed. He opened the door for the girl who hesitated before getting in the vehicle. She had beautiful green eyes, and they seemed to beg me to do something. I got another look at the tattoo, and I saw she was wearing a pendant around her neck - a locket of some kind. I didn't know what to say. I looked at Drew. He'd clenched his jaw as he watched the man walk around to his side of the vehicle. He sped out of the parking lot. I noticed the license plate - NCNTRL.

I wondered what he was in control of. The temperature was in the low 80s, but I felt a shiver down my spine. Drew stood there with his hands on his hips. He pursed his lips and didn't say anything as his eyes followed the car out of the parking lot. He shook his head and grabbed his cell phone. He turned so I couldn't hear the conversation. I knew he was calling someone about what we'd just seen, whatever that was.

I tried to shake off this sense of fear and dread I had for the young woman. She looked so young underneath a mask of makeup.

"Come on. Let's celebrate," said Drew as he finished his call. I tried to smile, but thoughts started to nag me. I knew she was in some sort of danger not that I could do anything about it. I hated feeling powerless.

Mick's was one of the few restaurants in town where the music over the sound system wasn't fighting with the sounds from the multiple televisions. In fact, there were no televisions or radios in Mick's, only the sounds of the live jazz trio. The alto singing Billie Holliday was peaceful. The cool candlelit room was refreshing. The hostess led us to a quiet table for two in the corner.

"I can't remember the last time we came here."

"Our anniversary two years ago," Drew shot back.

"Sometimes, I'm surprised at the things you remember."

"Grace Ward, I remember lots of things," he smiled and winked at me. I knew that smile too. I hadn't seen it in a while. "I especially remember important things concerning you like our anniversary, my proposal, and the day I saw you as more than Zack's little sister."

I wondered why he'd said that at first. It wasn't our wedding anniversary, and it wasn't the anniversary of the day he proposed. But it was close to the day years ago when he saw me as more than Zack's little sister. I usually couldn't forget that day either, but I realized how distracted I'd been. I was 13 when Drew stopped coming by the house to see Zack who went straight into the military after high school graduation. Drew could have done pretty much anything he wanted to. Drew graduated in the top five percent of his class, and he was an all-state football player. Those two ingredients, well, probably mainly the football, had a lot to do with him getting into the University of Georgia, but after a year at Georgia, he quit to follow what he'd always wanted to do - become a sheriff's deputy. When Drew returned to Augusta, Zack was in Iraq, where he did two tours. Zack missed several Christmases and Thanksgivings with us so Drew didn't come around. I tried to forget those blue eyes, but I couldn't. I was too shy to try and find a way to get in touch with him. My mother wouldn't have approved anyway. She always told me that a lady did not chase after a man.

I started attending classes at Augusta State University, hoping to get into the nursing program at the Medical College of Georgia. I wanted to save lives until I took a biology class my second semester, and we had to dissect animals. I lost my breakfast, and then I almost passed out. Fortunately, I made it to the ladies room in time, and I didn't die of embarrassment that spring day. I did, however, want to crawl under a rock and stay there. I was still lightheaded when I left school, and I probably shouldn't have gotten behind the wheel. I think Emmie tried to convince me not to drive, but it wasn't that far to our house. I thought I could make it safely. I was wrong. It wasn't a bad accident. I tapped the car in front of me at the light. I was already shaking, but when I saw who the officer called to the scene was, my hands shook even more. Despite the fact that it had been almost six years since I'd seen him, I knew him right away. He was even more handsome than I remembered. Dark hair and blue eyes. It was a good thing I wasn't standing. I think I went even weaker at the knees.

He didn't recognize me at first. When he asked for my driver's license and registration, he winked at me, but he still gave me a ticket. Later that afternoon after he got off work, he dropped by my house, and we sat on the front porch, talking for several hours into the evening under my mother's watchful eye. He was a frequent guest from that day on. I switched my major to business administration and graduated three years later. We got married six months after graduation, and here we were 10 years later. He took my hand as we sat in almost the same spot in the restaurant where he proposed. Although we didn't come here much, the restaurant always brought good memories with it. We needed some good memories right about now.

"Drew, I can't tell you how happy I am for you. I know this is something you've worked hard for all your life."

"And I couldn't have done it without you. You've been there the whole time."

"Your dad would've been proud."

He nodded. His father had been part of the sheriff's department for many years. He was killed in the line of duty two weeks before Drew was born. What he thought was a routine traffic stop turned out to be deadly. The suspect had been fleeing a yet undiscovered murder scene. His dad's dream was to be a detective, but he was still a few years short of it. Drew's mother tried to persuade her son not to attend the police academy, but her years of telling Drew how great a man his father was had created the picture of a hero in his young mind he couldn't shake. She'd created a shrine to her late husband, complete with photographs and framed newspaper articles.

"And I know that your mom is too."

"I called her right after I left your shop. And yes, the party is being planned, but it can't be for a couple of weeks. Something about some golf tournament," he said and then laughed.

"Wait, golf? You mean there's going to be a golf tournament here next week?"

We laughed because even though most of us locals didn't make it within the gates, the tournament consumed Augusta the first full week in April. You'd have to live under a rock not to know about it.

Drew and I hadn't spent a lot of time together in the past few months, and the time we did spent together was strained. We'd been drifting apart, and I didn't know how to bridge the gap. I tried to talk about the shop, but Drew was never really interested in flowers even though he tried to act that way. And I only knew about homicide from what I see on TV. Drew tried to shield me from things he knew from his job. While I struggled to think of something to talk about, I couldn't get my mind off that woman in the parking lot. I wasn't sure of her relationship to that man, but something wasn't right about it. With her eyes, she'd asked me for help, and I'd done nothing. Sometimes, I pick up things about people, but I thought that situation had to have been obvious to anyone watching. Emmie said I should have been a counselor or psychiatrist because people have always told me about their problems without me having to ask.

"Grace, what's wrong? We're supposed to be celebrating, and

you're someplace else."

"Nothing." I shook my head to emphasize the point.

"I'm not stupid. I've been married to you long enough to know when something's bothering you."

I looked up from my grilled shrimp and steak platter.

"Something about that couple we saw in the parking lot bothers me, Drew."

He nodded.

"I saw her eyes. She was afraid."

"I know. I made a couple of calls to be on the lookout for them, and a traffic violation may lead to something else. I don't know. Try not to think about it, okay?"

"I'll try. She just looked so scared, and I -"

I was about to say too much.

"And you what?"

"Nothing."

"Grace."

It was that low, authoritative voice.

"I saw her in my dream last night."

His jaw tightened as I said that, and he narrowed his eyes at me.

"I know she was scared, Grace, but they weren't breaking the law so there's nothing I can do. Let's just enjoy tonight."

"Whatever you want," I tried to smile, but it was hard. I was already on edge. "This evening is about you."

"No, babe. It's about us and our future. What would you like to do?"

"Let's take a walk down by the river."

"But don't you know it's dangerous down there?" he asked sarcastically.

"I've heard that rumor, but I have Augusta's best detective to take care of me. And you have a gun."

He smiled.

"That I do."

"So let's go for a walk. There's a jazz concert at 8. We can make it a jazz evening since we both love it."

"That sounds like a great plan, Mrs. Ward," he said and smiled.

We arrived at the river after the concert had started. By this time, the temperatures had dropped some. Good old Augusta springtime weather for you. It was dipping into the 50s. Drew gave me his sport coat to wear. A lot of people at the concert had brought blankets and lawn chairs, and several of them had picnics. We didn't have anything to sit on. Drew surprised me as he grabbed my hand instead.

"Could I have this dance?" he asked, pulling me close to him. I rested my head on his chest as we swayed in the cool breeze from the river. I hadn't seen his romantic streak in months. It had been buried by life.

After a few songs, we wandered along the Riverwalk to find a park bench. We could still hear the music.

"Grace, I'm sorry the last few months have been so hard. I know I've put in a lot of hours, but that's part of my job. I tried to warn you when you married me. I haven't intentionally been trying to ignore you. I know you've needed me, and I haven't been there."

I turned to look at him. The sun had set, but we were near a lamppost, and I could see his face in the pale light.

"I miss us and what we used to be to each other."

"We've been talking about taking a vacation for a while. Maybe it's time for us to do that."

"I've got a lot of weddings coming up, but Beth seems to enjoy being left in charge."

He kissed me.

"I think the concert is winding down, but we've got a great jazz collection at home we can dance to. What do you say?"

"That sounds like a great plan."

At home, he put on some smooth jazz and pulled me into his arms to dance.

"This is the perfect way to celebrate my promotion," he said as he kissed down my neck.

I fell asleep cradled in his arms. For one night at least, it was almost like the past few months had never happened. I was taken back to earlier years of our marriage. He was right it was a perfect ending to a perfect celebration until I was jolted awake at 3 a.m., that is. I dreamed of the young woman. Her feet and hands were bound, and her mouth was covered with silver duct tape. She was in a room all alone, and she was afraid. The light was on in the room, but the hallway I was in was dark. I could see into her room through a small window in the door. I tried to open it. It was locked. I started beating on the door. I shook it. Then I realized she wasn't alone. I saw a man walk toward her or maybe it was a woman. I couldn't tell. The person stood in front of her. I heard a single gunshot. I heard a thud to the floor. I screamed. The person turned toward me. I couldn't really see the face. It was dark, but somehow I knew it wasn't the same man I saw with her in the parking lot. I started to run and saw lots of the smaller rooms. Each of them had at least one young woman in it. As I passed, each one came to the door and pleaded with me to help them escape. They all had the same fearful expression as that of the first woman. I kept running because I knew someone was behind me. I could hear the sound of heavy footsteps getting closer. I heard the sound of a train whistle, and that's when I woke up. I could feel my heart pounding in my chest. A train was passing by a few blocks away. I wasn't sure if the train was in the dream or if it was the real whistle breaking through my sleep. Trains were common here. It was hard to live in Augusta without running into a set of train tracks somewhere along the way, and there always seemed to be a train at the most inconvenient times.

"Babe, what's wrong?" Drew sat up and put his arm around me as I tried to catch my breath.

I'd had dreams since I was a teenager. Sometimes, they scared me because they often came true. I'd had lots of dreams - some good, some bad. The last one I had that scared me like this....well, I didn't want to think of it. What happened after that dream combined with another I had were the reasons Drew and I were drifting apart. I couldn't think about that. What was I going to tell Drew? He'd always listened to me even when other people thought I was crazy, but he didn't want to hear about my dreams any more. He shut me off at the mention of the word. I really needed him to hear me out on this one though. I was shaking. I couldn't help it, but I started to cry.

"Grace, talk to me."

I shook my head.

"Go back to sleep, Drew."

My voice felt like it was lodged in my throat as an invisible set of hands blocked my airway. It was so real, as if I'd actually been there.

"Not until you tell me what's wrong."

I turned to look at him. I could see his face in the moonlight.

"I had a horrible dream. Something awful has happened to that woman in the parking lot. I know it. She's dead, Drew. I know she is."

His eyes narrowed at me, and I saw him clench his jaw.

"Babe, it wasn't real. You were just dreaming. You are worried about that girl, and your subconscious picked it up. It came out in a dream. I'll check in the morning to see if anyone heard anything."

His condescending tone made me angry.

"It's too late for her. But it might not be too late for the others."

"Others? What do you mean?"

"She's not the only one. I've read a lot of things about human trafficking. It can happen anywhere, and I'm not stupid. I know it happens here especially in April."

"You do remember who you're married to, right? You know what I do for a living. I've dealt with cases of it. I know it exists, and I know it exists here. But I'm homicide now. That's not my department."

I pushed away from him. I had to get out of bed. I couldn't go back to sleep for fear of going back into that dream.

"That's where you're wrong, Drew. She was murdered."

My voice shook as I said those words. I usually wasn't as forceful, but I knew what I'd seen.

"I need to go in the other room, Drew. I know you don't believe in my dreams any more, but it was real. And you know it."

He ignored my comment.

"Are you okay?"

"I'm fine, Drew, but they aren't. Just leave me alone."

I went into the living room and sank into the comfy, overstuffed chair. I had a journal that I wrote my dreams and their outcomes in. I picked it up and tried to shake the image of the imprisoned girls. I whispered desperate prayers for these young women. Human trafficking had been in the news a lot recently. There was an FBI sting in the state that netted a dozen arrests in Augusta. I'd heard that Atlanta was a hub for human trafficking. We're only two hours from Atlanta with one interstate connecting the two cities. A lot of people want to think it's only a big city problem or in other countries, but I knew it was big business in smaller towns too and large sporting events were a magnet for this type of activity. In April, Augusta becomes the center of attention in the golfing world with golfers and visitors coming from around the globe. It would be naive to think it didn't happen here at least in the spring, but we knew it wasn't just in the spring. We'd always made jokes about the women working the corners in downtown. Of course, it happened here. Like people in most places, we just chose to ignore it and them.

It didn't take Drew long before he came out into the living room with me. He grabbed my hand to help me up, and he led me to his chair. He sat down in the recliner, pulled me into his lap, and pushed the chair back so I could lie on his chest.

"You can't carry the world on your shoulders, baby. I know what you saw bothers you. I wish I could say it will be okay, but I can't. I know what the reality is."

"I wish there was something I could do."

"Babe, if there's more to this, I promise I'll get to the bottom of it. I'll go in in the morning and check around. Okay?"

I could only nod. He held me for a long time, and I fell asleep in his arms.

3

I woke up alone in Drew's chair. I couldn't remember him getting up and leaving me there. I felt like I'd been trampled on by a herd of wild buffalo. I dragged myself into the shop because it was going to be a busy day. I needed caffeine.

"You look terrible," Emmie greeted me at the door with a paper cup filled with sweet tea in hand. "I saw you pull in. You're never late. I thought you could use this."

"Thanks."

"Did you have a good night?"

Emmie was full of smiles. She liked to pry.

"Parts of it were good. We had a nice dinner and then caught the jazz concert on the river. Then, we danced at home."

"I love the jazz concerts. I'd go every week if I could," said Emmie.

"I know what you mean."

"What happened after that? Are things with you and Drew getting any better? Give me the juicy details."

"You're incorrigible. It was like we had no problems at all."

"That sounds good."

"Part of it seemed forced - like when your mother tells you to apologize to your brother and makes you hug him."

"I had a sister, and we always pinched each other during those hugs."

"See what I mean."

"Aw. Sweetie, it's just going to take time."

I simply nodded and tried to pass her to go to my office.

"What aren't you telling me?"

"Not much. The reason everything seemed to be fine with us is that I had a hard time paying attention to us. I think I was in my own little world last night, and I'm not sure Drew was there with me."

"What are you talking about?"

"I saw someone, and I know she's in danger. Then I had this awful dream. Two awful dreams, actually. They scared me."

"Did you tell Drew?"

"Drew was there last night when we met her. And I told him parts of my dream, but there's nothing he can do until a crime has been committed. In a way, I hope he doesn't have to do anything because that would mean a murder."

I took a sip of the tea. It was ice cold and sweet - just the way I liked it.

"Enough chit chat. We have two weddings today. Where's Beth?"

"I'm here, and we're ready to go," Beth said as she walked into the room.

"Really?"

"Yep, everything just needs to be loaded and taken to the churches and the 'closed' sign put on the door."

"Okay, Emmie and I can take my SUV and head to set up for the wedding at Riverwalk."

"See you later, Grace," said Beth.

The Riverwalk amphitheatre was directly on the Savannah River. I loved the river. It was peaceful at least, and I could relive part of my date with my husband. Dancing under the stars was magical, and for those moments, I think I blocked out the young woman's face and that butterfly tattoo. It was only supposed to be in the low 70s today, and the morning breeze was perfect as we placed flowers on the archway and two candelabra we'd brought for the wedding. I wasn't really paying attention to the decorating as much as I was gazing over the water. I watched as a few kayakers and canoeists glided over the river. I turned to follow them down the river until they were out of my sight. I decided to walk toward the river for a minute, leaving Emmie with the task of placing the flowers around the arch. As I did, more of the tree-lined river bank came into view. I noticed a group of people gathering near the water's edge and leaning over the green railings. I couldn't tell why. They seemed to be pointing at something. There was a shrill scream and then another.

Emmie ran up behind me.

"What's going on?" she asked.

Immediately, there was a sick feeling in the pit of my stomach as my dream flashed before me. My first thought was that woman. I couldn't really call her a woman. Even though she had a lot of makeup on, there was something about her that made her so young. She couldn't have been more than a teenager.

"I'm not sure, but I'm going to find out."

I rushed down the brick-covered pathway. I saw a woman with a black Labrador retriever on a leash, and a jogger, who kept jogging in place, as he lingered at the site. Several people stood back and pointed. A few people were taking photos on their phones. There were no police officers on the scene as I pushed past a few people toward the river's edge and saw the reason for the screams. As I peered over the railing, I could see a woman's body floating on the surface. She seemed to be tangled in something. And it wasn't just any woman. It was her - the woman who haunted my previous nights' dreams. I recognized her immediately. I couldn't scream; I felt numb and sick all at the same time. All I could do was stare. This couldn't be happening. I needed to call Drew. I fumbled for my cell phone which was in my pants' pocket. I was thankful he was in my contact list because I could barely remember his name much less his phone number. When he answered, I couldn't respond.

"Grace. Grace. Are you there?" Drew asked, but I couldn't form any words to answer him as I stared at the body. "Grace, talk to me.

Are you okay?"

I managed to force out the words through the air.

"Drew, it's her."

My voice sounded like it was in a cave. I guess it was me speaking. I wasn't sure. I knew I was thinking it. Did the words escape my mouth? I felt like I was choking on the words.

"What are you talking about? Who? Where are you?"

"Riverwalk. The girl from last night. She's dead. I'm looking at her body. She's face up in the Savannah River."

"Don't move. I'm on the way."

It was funny to me that he said not to move. I couldn't move if I tried. My feet felt like they had cement around them. Emmie linked her arm through mine. I couldn't break my gaze from the body as horrific as the scene was. I kept seeing the woman alive from the night before, alive, beautiful, and scared. I was grateful her eyes were closed. How was this possible? I'd only seen her hours before, and Drew and I had danced under the moonlight only yards away.

"Grace, you shouldn't be here."

Emmie's voice sounded so far away.

"Drew told me not to move. Emmie, it's her."

My cheeks felt wet as the breeze hit them. Was I crying? I touched my face. I couldn't believe what was going on. Within a few minutes, an officer on a motorcycle pulled up to the scene to secure it. He walked over to us.

"Grace, it's Butch. I need you and Emmie to step back."

I glanced at him, but it was almost as though he was speaking a foreign language. I knew Butch, didn't I? I guess I knew that Emmie was standing close to me, but everything felt strange. I felt like I was watching a movie or something. None of this could be real, could it? Emmie tugged on my arm to pull me away from the scene.

"There's a bench over there. Let's go sit down and wait for Drew. He's homicide, right?"

Homicide. That ominous word. Homicide. She was dead, and they didn't think it was an accident. I shouldn't be shocked, should I?

23

I knew this was going to happen. I saw it happen. The dream was so real, but this didn't seem real.

I glanced at Emmie. Her brow was furrowed. I could tell she didn't know what to do. Neither did I. I was caught between reality and my dream. Time had stopped. I could see what was going on, but at the same time, it couldn't have been happening. I had no idea how long it took Drew to arrive on the scene. It seemed like an eternity, but at the same time, he was quick. Nothing made any sense. When he arrived, I was still seated next to Emmie on the bench. More officers had gathered around the crime scene. I could see them putting up yellow tape and pushing the gawkers out of the way. Drew knelt in front of me and took both of my hands into his. I stared into his beautiful blue eyes. I wanted to tell him to wake me up from this nightmare.

"Babe," he said staring back at me.

I think I nodded. It was too hard to speak.

"We need to get a statement from you."

I shook my head.

"I can't."

"Grace, are you okay?"

"I saw this in my dream, Drew. I saw her in my dream. I knew she was in trouble, and I didn't help her."

I looked past him to see the other deputies on the scene. The yellow tape was around the area now. One deputy was taking photographs and a few others were scouring the area below for any evidence. They hadn't touched the body. In my mind, I could still see her bobbing in the water.

"Grace, look at me. This deputy is going to take your statement."

I was aware that another deputy had walked up behind Drew. I couldn't break my gaze from the crime scene.

"We should've done something, Drew. She needed us."

I couldn't look at him as I said it. I'd let her down. I didn't do anything when her eyes begged me to help her.

"Grace, I made calls. There wasn't anything else we could've done. I can't arrest someone on suspicion of a crime that hasn't taken place."

I looked at him. I hadn't noticed his face before now. The pain in his eyes. I saw it. It was worse than it had been. I reached out to touch his face for a moment before he stood up and turned to the deputy.

"This is my wife, Grace Ward," he said.

I wasn't sure what he said the deputy's name was. I was still in a haze.

Emmie moved away from the bench so Drew could sit next to me.

"Grace, I need you to tell me what happened here."

A statement. He wanted me to give a statement. I didn't know what I was supposed to say.

"Tell us about last night," Drew prompted.

The details of the previous night were burned into my mind. He put his arm around me as words spilled out of my mouth. I had rehearsed the events of the previous night over and over in my mind so many times that it sounded like a script I was reading.

When the deputy moved away, Drew touched my cheek to get my attention.

"Grace, there will be an autopsy, and we've got to search for clues. Whoever dumped the body did a lousy job. She got wrapped up in some of the vines or something and never sank," he said.

I looked down at the ground. I knew that. I'd seen it.

"We were on this river last night only a couple of blocks away, Drew."

My hands were shaking.

"I know."

I moved my glance to stare into his face. I had to see into his eyes.

"Drew, you said vice wasn't your department. Murder is. Now, you have to do something."

I couldn't hold back the emotion any more. I went from being stunned and dazed to being overwhelmed with tears. He held my hand and nodded.

"I will. I promise you. I will."

I knew he meant it. I just wished we could've saved her. He pulled me close and rocked me as I cried. I'm not sure how long I cried, but once the tears began to subside, he gently pushed me away so he could look into my eyes as he spoke.

"Listen, I don't know how long I'm going to be. I have a lot of things I have to do, and other witnesses to interview."

I nodded.

"I don't want you to be alone."

He turned to Emmie who'd walked away to make a phone call.

"Emmie, can Grace stay with you?"

"Of course, she can, sweetie. Blake has the boys this weekend so I'm alone."

He turned back to me.

"I have to get back to this now, but one more thing. Don't talk to any reporters."

"Okay."

I don't remember walking back to the vehicle. My feet moved without me being consciously aware of what was taking place. Emmie locked arms with me. If she hadn't held me up, I think my legs might have collapsed beneath me. They wobbled like jelly.

"I called Beth. She's going to take care of the next wedding for us. Everything is fine here although I wonder if the wedding will still take place now, but that's not up to us. I'm taking you to my house," Emmie said.

I was so grateful to Emmie. I was surprised at how well she was doing. Didn't seeing a dead body bother her?

We pulled up to Emmie's cute cottage. She lived in a small craftsman cottage in an older pine-tree lined neighborhood. It had two bedrooms, one bathroom, a living room, and a kitchen. But what made it worth it to Emmie was her backyard and her front porch with its swing and white wicker rocking chairs. It was a cute cottage. Ivy grew up the sides of the house, and she had several window boxes with red geranium. There was an old brick sidewalk lined on both sides with monkey grass. Emmie's house was quaint on the outside, but inside, it showed her eclectic flair for decorating. She had wonderful taste and had the artwork from several local artists and some of her own hanging on her walls.

My mind was all over the place. As I thought about Emmie, I wondered why she continued to work for me. She and Beth were only part-time employees, but they were both my lifelong friends. I wished I could hire them full time or at least hire Emmie full-time, but I didn't have enough business. When there were more weddings, I gave Emmie more hours. She worked another part time job to support her two small boys. At least the split with her ex was amicable, and he did pay child support on time every month. It helped Emmie stay afloat, but Emmie didn't have a lot of time to devote to what she really loved, which was painting. She was an amazing visual artist, and from time to time, she'd show her work in venues around town. If she didn't have two children to care for, she would 've had no problem going the "starving artist" route. Before she met her ex-husband, she lived in a warehouse, where she painted her days away and was happy.

Beth, on the other hand, didn't necessarily need a job at all. Her husband was an obstetrician, and he was a silent partner in several businesses earning lucrative side income. Beth used her time in the floral shop as her creative outlet. Beth had a fulltime nanny for her 3 year-old twins.

I heard Emmie's words breaking through my dazed state.

"You need something to drink, and since you don't drink alcohol, your choices are lemonade and sweet tea."

"Either would be great."

I sat on her front porch swing and stared in front of me. There was a massive oak tree, which provided an abundance of shade, in Emmie's front yard. It was a beautiful spring day. I could hear the mourning doves cooing and saw a few butterflies flitting by.

Emmie returned with two clear glasses of lemonade.

"Here you go, honey," she said, handing me one.

"Excuse me," Emmie and I turned at the sound of the voice to see a woman coming up the walkway.

Emmie stepped forward.

"Yes?"

"I'm with the news radio station. I saw you at the river this morning."

"I'm sorry. We can't talk to you."

"Please. It won't take long."

"No, we can't," Emmie pushed me inside her house.

I was shaking. I could hear Drew's voice in my mind, sternly telling me not to talk to any reporters. I wondered if there would be others who might try to ask me questions.

"Okay. So what's going on? You didn't tell that deputy everything when you gave your statement, did you? I couldn't hear all of what you said."

I sat on Emmie's overstuffed couch and drew my knees to my chest, wrapping my arms around them. I didn't say anything as Emmie sat down. Emmie stared at me waiting for me to say something.

"My dream last night. The girl in the parking lot. It was the same girl."

"I gathered that. What did Drew have to say about all of this?"

"I told him about my dream early this morning when I woke up from it. It scared me, and I sat straight up in the bed. He doesn't really want to hear about my dreams, but it was so real. I felt like I was there, and I could feel all of their fear. The helpless feeling was the worst part, though. I couldn't do anything. It was horrible."

"It's not like this is the first time this has happened."

"I know, but I wish it didn't happen at all. I guess it's a gift, but I feel this is a curse sometimes. It's just that it brings up memories in Drew of places he'd rather not go."

"It really is a gift. You don't always know bad stuff and knowing you, I bet you don't tell people half of what you dream about."

I laughed at that comment. If she only knew. There were plenty of times I'd kept my mouth shut, and I later kicked myself because my dream might have prevented a negative outcome. I dreamt that a friend had a car accident. The road and time of day were specific. I told her, and she started taking a different route home from work. A few weeks later, there was a horrible accident on that road at the precise time she would have been on it. But not all of them had happy endings. There was this dead girl, and I saw it happen.

"You've had some beautiful dreams too. I think you've had more good ones than bad."

"True, but people tend to remember the bad."

"No. Drew is remembering the bad. You've been right about a lot of things. And even though I didn't want to hear it, I was glad when you told me about your dream with Blake and Cindy. I suspected it, but when you said it, it made me confront him. I didn't want to live with someone who was only staying with me just for the kids' sake. I wanted to be with someone who loved me for me. But you also had a dream that I'd have another baby after Jake was stillborn. I know you didn't want to tell me at the time, but it meant so much to me. It gave me hope. It wasn't like Luke was a replacement, but it made me not afraid to try again."

"Thank you. I never know what to do with some of this stuff, Emmie. Church people think I'm weird, and I've never really fit in with them even though I believe God's behind what I know."

"Not all church people think you're strange. I was the one who ended up delivering the arrangement to Dana Andrews last night. The hospital was on the way - well in a roundabout way. I was closer than Beth. Besides, I wanted to see the baby," Emmie smiled. "I took it directly to her room since I know her. She was disappointed that you didn't bring it. She asked me about you, but I told her about Drew's promotion instead. She said you'd had a dream about her and a little girl years ago. I think she said she'd been holding onto that for nearly eight years."

I felt myself nodding. I was still numb.

"I can't talk about Dana, okay?"

"I understand. I think it's just that you are sensitive to other people, and that comes through in your dreams. Being sensitive and compassionate is a God-given gift. More people should have it," said Emmie. "And I know it's hard for you to tell people sometimes because you wonder what they think about you, but there are several people whose lives you've impacted and you don't even realize it."

"Sometimes. People have always thought I was strange though. They stayed away from me. You and Beth and -" I started to say Dana, but I wasn't sure. "You and Beth are the only friends I have, and most of the time, I can't figure out how I'm friends with Beth."

We both laughed at that comment.

"She's changed since high school," said Emmie. She wrinkled her nose then laughed. "Okay. Her hairstyle is different."

"The hair definitely, but the personality never."

"I guess she must grow on you after a while?"

"Mold will also grow on something after a while."

Emmie laughed.

"Oh, we know she's not that bad. She's really only abrasive to the people she's comfortable with. She doesn't feel the need to put up her walls or her 'Mrs. Dr.' face, and she speaks freely."

"That's true. She doesn't pull any punches, and maybe we could learn a thing or two from her. I wish I could be as bold as she is."

"That's true, but she does have a soft side. She helped me through that rough patch when I had to take time off after Dylan's appendicitis, and my car broke down on top of everything. Blake was great, but I didn't expect him to pay my bills. And I never told anyone I was having a hard time except you. I know it was Beth who put a few bills in an envelope and shoved it under my front door. She was so embarrassed when I hugged her the next time I saw her. You should've seen the look on her face. I think I saw a tear before she looked away."

"Sounds like Beth. Listen, Emmie, I've been so busy with

weddings this week that I forgot to tell you and Beth. I have ins with a couple of new caterers, and I've got several parties we are doing flowers for. There are some big orders including a champions' dinner at one of the houses."

When the golfers and visitors came to town for the tournament, they typically rented homes in some of the more prestigious parts of town. It was a tradition that dated back as long as anyone could remember. During the week, there were often lavish get-togethers. I was looking forward to what the week might mean for business.

"That's exciting."

"Hopefully, it will mean some bonuses for you."

Emmie smiled.

"Sweetie, I appreciate everything you do for me. I love working with you, and I know it's going to get better. But you know Beth is all about the parties that week."

"Yes, that's why I'm probably going to need you a lot that week. Do you think you can do it?"

"Actually, that's Blake's week, and they are going to take the boys to Florida. It works out perfectly."

"Is there anything else you want to talk about?" Emmie asked.

I shook my head.

"I think I'm talked and cried out at this point. I'm grateful to have been so busy lately. Since you and Beth are only available a few days during the week, I'm so glad that I have to force myself to go into the shop every day. It's kept me sane, and being around the beautiful flowers calms my soul. Plus you wouldn't believe how many people come in just to talk; sharing in their happiness and even sometimes in their sorrow has been a big help to me."

"Sounds like someone needs a hug," Emmie said and put her arms around me before I knew what was going on. "You would've made a great counselor."

"You say that a lot, but taking psychology was so depressing in college. It made me wonder if this was an illness that could be fixed. I don't think Drew will be finished any time soon. Do you mind if I stay here tonight? I'd rather not be alone."

A broad grin came over Emmie's face.

"Girls night!" she exclaimed. "Of course, it will be fun to have a girls' night in. We could have an old-fashioned sleep over. Horror movies and ice cream?"

"We saw a dead body this morning. That's enough horror to last me a lifetime. I can't get her face out of my head. And what's the deal with you? How are you so calm during this?"

"Don't you remember when my parents tried to force me to get a real job? After you ran out of biology and threw up in the ladies' room, I stuck it out for a few more semesters, but at Augusta Tech instead. I thought about being a paramedic, but after a couple of nights on an ambulance, I saw some gruesome stuff and some dead bodies. I knew I couldn't do that for a living. I had your biology class experience on the side of the road one night. It took a lot of pages in my sketchpad to get through that."

I nodded.

"Well, I'm glad it happened to me. Otherwise, I might have been okay to drive home. Who would've thought that me being grossed out in biology would've changed my life forever?"

"You would've wound up with him anyway. I think you two were always supposed to be together. I still remember the first time I saw you with Drew. I was so jealous of you."

"Really?"

"Are you kidding me? Those eyes; those biceps," she had a huge grin on her face as she winked at me. "What a hottie."

"Emmie," I tried to fake being outraged with her for saying that, but I laughed instead. She knew how to get my mind off the things that were bothering me.

"What? As long as I'm not telling him that I think he's a hottie, we're okay. Besides, he still only has eyes for you despite what you think."

"Love conquers all?"

"When you are in love with someone, you just don't give up

on them. And you two are still madly, deeply in love with each other. You can't see it right now, but everyone else who loves you can. And whatever is going on with you will be resolved. I know that about you okay? You have dreams, but I can see what's staring me in the face."

I hoped she was right. I knew I still loved Drew, but his actions sometimes made me wonder about his feelings for me. On some days, it was crystal clear, but on others, it wasn't.

"Now that I've gotten your mind off other things, how about some chick-flicks and ice cream."

Emmie held up several DVD cases of well-known tear-jerkers.

"Where are the tissues?"

"I think we might need a case of them if we watch all those," I said.

"This is going to be a mucus-filled night."

She didn't even look up when she said that. She sounded so serious that I couldn't help but laugh. My giggles spurred Emmie's. If Emmie was anything, she was spontaneous and unpredictable.

"That is so gross, Emmie. How old are you?"

I threw one of her pillows from the couch at her.

"What? I'm the mother of two boys. Besides, you haven't had a good cry until your nose joins in and cries too."

She laughed, and I had to laugh with her because I'd never heard it put that way before. She was right. I knew where this night was headed, but it didn't have anything to do with chick flicks. I had a feeling we'd be watching cornball comedies before it was all said and done. It was definitely going to be a Marx Brothers or Abbott and Costello type of night.

"You're right, Emmie. What kind of ice cream do you have?"

"Mint chocolate chip and chocolate chip cookie dough, of course."

"My favorites. Emmie, have I ever told you that you are my hero?"

"Well, not lately, but I have saved you a few times, haven't I?"

"More than you know."

4

It's a good thing we stayed up and watched movies all night. After one movie with lots of tissues, we shifted to some Lucille Ball, Abbott and Costello and even some newer stuff. I wouldn't have been able to sleep anyway. I kept trying to get the images of her frightened face and then her dead face out of my head. Somehow we made it to Sunday morning service. We sat in the back row and ducked out as quickly as we could. When I returned home, my house was empty. Everything was as it had been when I'd left the day before. If Drew had been there, there would have been evidence. About five minutes after I walked in, so did he.

"Hi."

He didn't respond verbally but walked straight toward me and pulled me into his arms. He held me close to him.

"What's wrong?"

"I missed you, and I'm sorry you had to see what you saw."

He kissed me and then sat down on his recliner. He looked a scruffy because it had been at least 24 hours since he shaved. His hair was disheveled. He'd come in with a partially loosened tie that he pulled the rest of the way off.

"It just reinforced why I didn't go into health care."

I tried to make light of it, and he gave me a weak smile.

"Where've you been? You look terrible."

"I stayed in my office all night. I ended up falling asleep at my desk. When I woke up, I came home. I tracked down clues yesterday. The license plate we saw belonged to a stolen car. Back in January, an 80 year-old man was found dead in his house. He had an immaculate 1957 Chevy in his garage with that license plate. The autopsy couldn't find any signs of foul play. He only has one nephew who reported the car stolen. He hinted that he thinks his uncle was murdered because of the locked garage he kept the car in. The car hasn't been recovered, and there are no leads to prove that his death was a murder. No trauma of any kind to the body. The car was the only thing missing."

"That sounds like a car collector's dream."

He nodded.

"You definitely couldn't take it down to a car lot and sell it without raising some suspicions."

"Is that murder connected to this girl. Who is she?"

"I'm trying to figure out if there is a connection. The nephew let us look around the place today. Nothing. The house is empty. It's on several acres of land. There's an old stable on the grounds. It was converted into another garage. Apparently, he had several vehicles at one time, but he sold all of them except the Chevy. It seemed to be a random theft, but now it's looking suspicious."

Drew shook his head.

"Everything we followed yesterday was a dead end. The crime lab is backed up so who knows how long it will be before toxicology tests are finished. They took DNA, but who knows if there's anything to match it with. We were hoping for an ID with dental records because there was nothing on the body, but several of her teeth were missing - like the killer pulled them. We could tell it had been done recently. Some of her skin -"

Drew paused and looked at my face. I winced. It was too horrific for me to think of.

"What about her tattoo?" I choked out the question.

Drew narrowed his eyes.

"You saw her tattoo?"

"I noticed it when she was talking to the man. He was holding her wrists, and it was on her left forearm. When you started talking to them, he let go of her wrist, and she pulled her arms to her chest. The tattoo was of a pink butterfly. It seemed to be really ornate, but I didn't want to stare. Didn't I mention that when I was giving my statement?"

"No, you didn't mention it, but you were in such a state of shock I'm surprised you remembered your name. I saw the tattoo, but I didn't get a good look at it. I was looking at his face more than her arm. But I thought maybe my eyes had played tricks on me after I read the preliminary coroner's report."

"What are you talking about?"

"Some of her skin was missing so there was no mention of the tattoo. Whoever killed her didn't want anyone to ID her - ever."

I sat down on the couch next to his chair.

"They cut her skin off?"

"'I'm not sure 'cut' is the right word. The coroner looked at the skin. He said he wasn't totally sure, but he thinks it may have been some type of corrosive acid used to burn off the tattoo and most of her forearm. Her fingerprints were wiped too."

I put my hand over my mouth. I started feeling nauseated. I'd heard of people throwing up after seeing dead bodies. I was so in shock yesterday that I don't think I processed all of my emotions, but as he kept talking, the room became stuffy. I started to feel hot, and I thought I might get sick if he kept describing her. I was still tired from having stayed up all night at Emmie's and from the night before that one. I got up. I needed some air or water or something. I headed into the kitchen, and Drew followed. I stood at the sink staring out into the back yard. Drew stood beside me and handed me a glass for some water.

"Are you okay?" Drew asked.

"No, I'm not okay. I feel sick. Why would someone do this?"

"I don't know, but I promise you, I will find out."

"How did she die?"

"There will be an autopsy to determine the cause, but she had a bullet wound to the chest."

"Why would the killer go through all that trouble to make sure she's never identified, but then be so careless about allowing the body to be found?"

Drew tilted his head at me.

"That's a good question, and one I don't know the answer to."

He got quiet for a few minutes as he seemed to be lost in a thought. I wanted to kick myself though for leaving out information when I gave my statement.

" I can't believe I didn't mention that tattoo. It was so beautiful, stunning. She pulled her arms close to her chest. She moved around some so I could see different angles of it, and she dropped her arm when she got into the car."

"I wish I'd gotten a closer look at it. It might be our only way of identifying our Jane Doe."

"What about the man she was with?"

"We're looking for someone to fit that description, but a lot of men fit that description," he said.

"He's not the one who killed her, but he probably knows who did."

That slipped out. I didn't mean to say it, and Drew narrowed his eyes at me after I did.

"Your dreams are not hard evidence," he snapped at me and looked away.

"Maybe not, but I know he wasn't the one who killed her," I snapped back without thinking.

Our date was nice, but it appeared we were heading back to our recent normal. I was going to chalk it up to stress and the fact that neither of us had slept in two days. My mind started to wander as I stared out the window. I really needed to plant some flowers. It was an overgrown mess out back. I took a deep breath.

"Are you hungry? Have you eaten anything?"

"I'm fine. I grabbed a biscuit on the way home. How was your time with Emmie?"

"We watched a tear-jerker then a bunch of slapstick, old-school comedy. I'd say that was a good day and night We didn't really sleep. Emmie always knows how to get a smile out of me."

"I'm glad. I'm sorry I snapped at you."

Drew paused. I could tell he wanted to say something. Whenever he was thinking about how to properly word something he'd wrinkle his forehead and sigh. The longer the sigh the harder the struggle.

"You said that tattoo was ornate?" he asked although I was pretty sure that wasn't what he wanted to ask me.

"Yes, it was beautiful, and it covered her entire forearm. It wasn't like a front view of a butterfly. It was more like a side view or maybe that's just the part I saw. I guess it could've covered her entire arm. Since that dress had no sleeves, I could see her arm well. I didn't want to stare though."

"There are a couple of tattoo artists in town. Do you think that maybe you would be able to recognize it if you saw it?"

"Absolutely."

"Grace, I need a favor."

"Why do you say it like that?"

"Because I need you to help me."

"You know I'll help you."

"We're going to have to go to a couple of tattoo places. I know you can be a little squeamish when it comes to needles, and someone might be getting one done while we're there."

"Oh. Well, I can just look away or something."

"I need to take a quick shower. Would you do an internet search to see if you find a similar looking butterfly? We can print it out and give them something to go on."

"Sure."

It didn't take me long to find a photograph of a blue swallowtail butterfly, which was the closest thing I could find to the image in the tattoo. Hers was bright pink though. I found two pictures. One was a side view of the butterfly in flight, and one was a full-on view. He was right about taking a quick shower. The images were still printing when he emerged from our room.

"So what did you come up with?" he asked.

I showed him the first picture.

"It may have been the angle of her arm, but all I saw was one wing of the butterfly. It covered most of her arm. At the bottom of this butterfly, there's a straight piece with a rounded tip. On her tattoo, the ends were curved instead of straight. Like a swirly design or an initial. Yes, it was an initial. Maybe a 'c' and an 's.' And there was a date. I knew I was staring. I tried to look away. I just couldn't. Also, the butterfly was edged in black, but the wings were a deep pink like fuchsia. That's not the natural color of this particular type of butterfly. "

"Great. I hope this was done locally."

The first stop was Lady Luck Ink, where Drew knew the owner. James was in the process of tattooing a bald eagle on the shoulder of a young man. He already had several tattoos including an American flag on his back.

"Hey, James. Could I ask you a couple of questions?"

"Sure, Drew. Can I finally talk you into a tattoo?" he laughed. Drew shook his head.

"This lady right here doesn't want me to have any of those, but this is official business. Have you put any butterflies on anyone lately?"

"What does it look like?"

"We don't have a photo of the actual tattoo," he said handing him the printout of the butterfly. "It's similar to this design but pink and with some lettering."

James shook his head.

"Not lately. A new group arrived at Fort Gordon not too long ago, and I've been doing a lot of flags and eagles."

Drew looked at me and nodded. I described it in a little more detail.

"It was bright pink and a couple of initials were part of the butterfly's design. Maybe the letters 'c' and 's.'"

James shook his head as he listened.

"It's not familiar to me, and it doesn't sound like the work of Red at Augusta Ink or Eddie at Lines of Ink either, but you could check with them."

"If you have any ideas, give me a call?" Drew asked.

"You bet. You sure you don't want one, Drew? I'm almost finished with this one. I could fix you up."

Drew winked at me, and I shook my head.

"You mean I can't have 'I love Grace' in a heart?" he asked with a big grin.

I smiled.

"You don't have to tattoo it on yourself to let me know that you love me."

"Good come back," Drew replied. He turned to James. "Here's my card just in case."

"No problem, and congrats on the promotion, man. You're good for this town."

"Appreciate that."

Drew didn't say anything as we walked back to the car. When we got in, he stared in front of him.

"Someone out there knows who this girl was. Let's try Augusta Ink and Lines of Ink."

Our questions at the two other tattoo businesses yielded the same response - blank looks and shaking heads. All we got from it was that it was an expensive tattoo. Most of the drive back home was quiet. A few blocks from the house, Drew broke the silence.

"I'm at a dead end. I've only been a homicide detective for two days. I can't have my first case end up being a cold case for some rookie detective to pour over and solve 20 years from now."

"I'm sure it's not a dead end. Would you -" I caught myself before I said anything else.

"Would I what?"

I hesitated trying to come up with something to say.

"Would you like to get something to eat?"

"Don't change the subject, Grace."

"Who said I was changing the subject?"

I tried to laugh it off. I wasn't in the mood for an argument. I watched his jaw tighten as he spoke, and he gripped the steering wheel tighter.

"I'm hungry."

"It's about that dream of yours, isn't it?"

We stopped at a light, and he turned to look at me.

I glanced out the window. He used to listen to my dreams. He used to place value in many of the things I said. Now, he bristled when I told him about them. I wouldn't have said anything about this one except that it woke me up with such violent force, and I was living it. If only, he'd listen to me.

"No, I really am hungry. All we had was ice cream."

"Grace, you know psychic phenomena is not valid evidence."

"I'm not a psychic , and you know it."

"It doesn't matter. What you are telling me is not something I can base on investigation on."

I was glad we were almost home.

"I'm going to take a nap," said Drew as he walked into our two-bedroom cottage. It was a lot like Emmie's place with a picturesque front porch in a quiet, older neighborhood in town.

I waited on the porch for a few minutes. I didn't want him to see I was upset, and I could tell he was upset with me. From the screened door, I watched him. Before he headed to the bedroom, he poured himself a glass of something - a full glass of something. I wasn't sure what it was - whiskey, bourbon. It didn't seem to matter these days. I was surprised though. He usually didn't drink in front of me and never in the middle of the day. I wasn't sure how much he drank. The bottle always seemed to stay about half full. I knew he was drinking at night because I could smell it on his breath. Once he threw that one back, two more quickly followed. I turned away. I couldn't watch him. I wasn't sure how anyone could drink that fast.

I sat helplessly on the front porch swing and thought about the man I knew and the man he was becoming. Drew had vowed long before we started dating to never to touch the stuff, which made his drinking much harder for me to understand. He told me once that he didn't drink because he'd seen so many lives destroyed. His earliest duties with the sheriff's department were traffic related. He told me about one wreck in which a man was driving down the expressway with his son and two other boys in the back of a pickup truck. The man had been drinking, and when he lost control, the three young boys were thrown from the truck. The man walked away, but the boys, all under the age of 12 died from their injuries. Two died instantly. The other one lingered at the trauma unit for a couple of days. Drew was there to watch as they put the boys' broken bodies into body bags.

He'd also worked on domestic violence calls and had seen women beaten to a bloody pulp by their alcoholic boyfriends or husbands. I'll never forget his face when he came home one night not long after we got married. It was pale. No. It was worse that pale. It was a deathly, ashen gray. He looked so much older than his 28 years that night a decade ago. His face fell, and wrinkles appeared where there'd been none before. He walked in and without a word held me tightly. Later I found out a woman had died. She'd been shot by her husband after Drew got a domestic violence call. It was a hostage situation, and he heard the shots ring out. The man killed her then turned the gun on himself. Only a few nights before Drew had been to the same house. The woman had refused to press charges against her husband after he'd beaten her so brutally that her eyes were swollen shut. The couple had a 2 year-old child who had seen the whole thing and was now an orphan. The image of the child screaming and covered in his parents' blood as he was taken out of the house stayed with Drew. I knew he still had nightmares about it. The dead husband was an alcoholic with a laundry list of substance abuse charges. Drew felt powerless to help them, and I knew he blamed himself for her death at least. Those were a couple of the worst cases I remember him telling me of, but there were more.

Deep down, I knew the hardest things about this for me were realizing my invincible husband wasn't as invincible as either of us thought, and that nothing I tried to do helped him. Sometimes, I wondered if I made matters worse. Right now, Drew only seemed to drink when he wanted to sleep. I wondered what would happen when it no longer helped or he decided he needed it to make it through his day.

After several minutes, I walked inside and stood at the bedroom door. He was out cold. I said a quick prayer under my breath. I wanted to help him. While he slept, I decided I could put my energy into finding a killer rather than being sad about things I couldn't change.

I took a deep breath and went back into the living room, where I picked up the notebook next to the couch. I'd written down details of the dream. What little details I had anyway. I didn't see the face of the person who shot the woman. I really wanted to give her a name. I knew the police were calling the victim "Jane Doe." Blonde hair and young. Who was she? Were the initials part of her name? C and S? Or it could have been an "L." Maybe it was a tribute to a friend who'd died too soon.

I decided to play detective on my own. The butterfly tattoo held the key to learning who the victim was. I knew I could spot the tattoo if I saw it again. I thought it was distinctive enough. I sat down at our computer and started searching social network sites for photos. Whoever had created the design had to be proud of it, and I was sure if the girl had a social media presence, there would be something linking the tattoo to her.

Butterflies seemed to be a common design, and there were even lots of pink ones. But this one was not like any of the rest. I wondered if the young woman had other tattoos. I guess Drew would've mentioned that. When that search came up dry, I decided to look for web pages of tattoo artists in the Southeast, but I found so many that I had to narrow it down even further. I started with tattoo artists in the bigger cities of Atlanta, Savannah and Macon in

Georgia. I accessed several websites and flipped through thumbnails of photographs. It was a long process. I lost track of the time, and although I spent most of the day searching, I didn't come up with anything.

"Do you know what time it is, Grace?" I heard a groggy voice behind me.

I glanced at the bottom of the screen. How could it be after midnight? I'd been at the computer since the early afternoon. I was glad he slept even if it had been longer than a nap.

"What are you up to?" he asked.

"Just playing on the computer. Nothing exciting."

I tried to cover my tracks by clicking to the other screen with the game of solitaire and swiveled the chair around so my back was to the computer. He pulled up a chair facing me.

"I've been standing here for a while. I know what you were doing."

"Then why bother asking?"

He didn't seem pleased with that remark.

"Talk about a needle in a haystack. I did a search for butterfly tattoos, but I didn't see anything like hers. Then, I started pulling up page after page of photographs. There are some really talented people out there."

"Does that mean you want to get a tattoo now?" he grinned at me, knowing I wasn't about to get a tattoo, but I thought I'd play along.

"How about I get one of those barbed wire ones across the small of my back?"

I watched for his reaction. He raised an eyebrow at me.

"Sexy, but I see you as more of the hearts and flowers on your ankle type," he said and laughed.

"You don't think I'm sexy?"

"Oh, you're extremely sexy, but only with me."

He moved a chair close to mine and sat down.

"Well, you would be the only one to see the barbed wire tattoo."

"Actually how about one that says 'I love Drew' on your tricep."

I shook my head. He was being ridiculous now, and we both knew it. I giggled at the thought.

"No, I think I'm good."

"Aw. I was starting to like the idea especially of the barbed wire."

"I'm sure you were."

He laughed, but it didn't take long for him to be serious once again.

"Grace, I appreciate your help."

I took a deep breath.

"But?"

"But I asked you to do what I needed you to do. There are other people who can help me with the rest."

"I didn't have anything else to do this evening, and I want to know who she was. I want to help you. I want her killer found."

He reached out for my hand.

"I want to find her killer too," he said. "I'll see if someone can do a search in the office tomorrow. Why don't you come to bed? When is the last time you slept?"

I shrugged my shoulders.

"You and I both need some."

I nodded. I would stop for now, but I think we both knew I'd return to my search when he wasn't around.

5

Drew only slept a few more hours before leaving for work at 4 a.m. I couldn't sleep. I was afraid of what I'd dream. I didn't open the shop until 9 o'clock, and with him gone, I had about four hours to find that tattoo on the Internet. I went through dozens of photographs of tattoos from web pages with no luck. I did have a computer at the shop. I would probably have time to continue the search once I got there depending on how many babies had been born on Sunday and how many funerals were scheduled for the week. Monday's workload was never predictable.

With the tournament the next week, I had to make sure I had enough flowers to create the arrangements for the events I had committed to.

I'd only been open for about 30 minutes when a couple walked in. I guessed them to be in their 50s. He was balding, and the woman had short, dark hair with a few strands of gray glistening through.

"Hi. Can I help you?"

"I hope so," he said. "My name is Ken, and this is my wife, Janice. We're part of a non-profit organization near Atlanta called 'Hope from the Night.' We help women get out of human trafficking."

I felt my mouth drop as I listened to them.

"A lot of people don't think it happens in their backyard," said Janice. "They think it happens in places like Thailand or somewhere overseas. Or if it happens in the U.S., it must be in California or New York. But Atlanta is a huge hub because of all of the conventions and sporting events that take place there. This type of business is a byproduct of the influx of visitors. Many of these women don't want to be involved in it, but once they are in, they can't get out. Some start as young as 13 as a way to survive. They live in fear of being raped or murdered. Many of them have drug addictions. They can't pull themselves out alone."

I leaned against the counter to steady myself. I couldn't believe what was happening. First, seeing the woman alive and knowing there was something wrong, then the dream, and now these people show up from out of nowhere. I knew human trafficking was involved. It was all coming together, but why me? Why was I involved in this? Of course, I've always wanted to do something important with my life. Maybe now I could?

I cleared my throat.

"I've read a lot of things about it. There have been a few FBI stings here with people getting arrested for child pornography and prostitution rings."

"Yes, there were a lot of people involved in that last one."

"I think there were almost as many from Augusta arrested as there were in Atlanta."

"You're probably right about that one," said Ken. "Well, then you must know that with all of the visitors who come here one week out of the year, the opportunists bring women here in hopes of scoring a lot of easy cash."

"I believe it. What can I help you with?"

Help. I wasn't able to help Jane Doe, but maybe I could help someone else.

"Well, in Atlanta, we have teams that go out at night. We talk to women and men who are involved in prostitution. We give them flowers as a symbol of hope, and we give them our phone number. We have programs set up to help them get education, jobs, new lives. Many of these women also have children. We help them break the cycle of addiction and abuse."

"Flowers, I can definitely help you with."

"We aren't asking you to give them to us. We'll pay you for them, but we want to know if you are too busy next week to help us. The florist we've used in the past has gone out of business, and everyone else is too busy."

"No, I'm not too busy. Tell me what you think you will need, and I'll do what I can."

"Great," said Ken.

"So where are you staying next week? The hotels are full."

"I'm from here," said Janice. "My sister and brother still live in the area so some of our team members will stay with them."

"Where will you give out the flowers?"

"We've talked to a lot of people to try to find out where these women might be trafficked. There are a couple of hotels that are our targets, and we've heard of a couple of parties where women's company is in the top billing to get people to come. Don't worry. We have our sources, and the less you know, the better for you."

"It sounds like this could be dangerous for you."

"We've had a few scares, but we've seen some successes in the 10 years we've been volunteering with this organization. That makes everything worth it."

"Count me in. I like to help people if I can. Flowers seem to make things better, don't you think?"

"Sometimes, we see a lot of tears when we give flowers to these young women. No one has ever given them a flower before. It's a small gesture to let them know we care."

"Well, you don't have to convince me."

"Great. Here's what we need, and here's my number," Ken handed me a business card.

"Here's my business card. Thank you."

"Coming here just felt right," said Janice. "It's nice meeting you, and we look forward to talking with you again soon."

I stared at the door for several minutes after the couple left, and then I gazed at the business card. I didn't believe in coincidences. With their visit, I was even more convinced my dream was real and there was some type of human trafficking activity that would take place next week. Maybe this was my chance to really help people. I couldn't be a nurse, but this might help save lives. As I was taking all of this in, I heard Emmie's voice.

"Good morning," she said.

"I didn't expect to see you today."

"I'm glad to see you too."

"That's not what I meant. You don't have to be here."

"I know, but there's a reason I came. I don't know why I didn't think about this sooner. When you sent me the text about the tattoo, I thought I could help."

"What do you mean?"

"Only that I can draw it for you," she said patting the floral canvas bag she was carrying. She placed it on the counter and pulled out her sketch pad and her pastels.

"You're brilliant, Emmie. I wish I could pay you what you're worth."

She smiled.

"Tell me what this tattoo looks like."

Emmie was amazing. As I watched her create the design that had been seared in my mind for the past few days, I couldn't believe how talented she was. I mean, I'd seen her work, but this was beyond what I thought she could do. From my description, she created the exact image I'd seen played through my brain.

"That's it. That's exactly what I saw. You're incredible. I don't know what to say."

"Just find out who she was and catch a killer for me."

I couldn't help but stare at the drawing.

"This may be asking too much, but do you think you could draw the guy she was with?"

"Are you kidding me? Of course, I can," she replied.

I described him to her and within a matter of minutes, she'd drawn him. It was like looking at a photograph.

"Emmie, you are incredible."

"Are you busy this morning?" Emmie asked.

"I have a couple of orders to fill, but this couple came in."

I handed Emmie their card.

"I saw something about this from an Atlanta TV station. Someone posted it online. They have a huge success rate. I wonder what it all means?"

"I don't know. Should I tell Drew?"

"Should you tell Drew what?"

I heard my husband's voice behind us. Emmie and I had our backs to the door so we didn't see Drew come in. The door chime hadn't worked in a few weeks.

I turned and gave him a hug.

"I thought you weren't coming by until lunch?"

"When you get to the office at 4:30, 10:30 is lunch," he said.

"Is it that late already?"

He nodded.

"You really need to get that door chime looked at, Grace," he said.

"That's on my to-do list, I promise."

I tried to skip over that one. He'd been after me for a couple of weeks about the door chime. I showed him Emmie's sketches.

"This is the tattoo, and this is the guy she was with."

"Emmie, these are amazing," he said as he stared at each of the drawings. "From your reaction, Grace, I take it you've been busy this morning."

"Busy, yes, but not working on flower orders."

"Do you have a lot of orders, sweetie?" Emmie asked.

"Just a couple, but Danny will be here shortly to deliver them. I got sidetracked."

"I'll help. I don't have to pick up Luke from PreK until 12:30."

"Thanks."

"I'm going to take this sketch back to the office."

"Do you have any news?"

"No, I wish I did. Toxicology reports can take months, and since she's a Jane Doe, there's no telling how long it might be. "

"She's not a Jane Doe. She's somebody."

I was angry that he couldn't find out who this person was.

"Grace, honey, I told you my first case isn't going to end up cold. I'm going to find out who she is," he said. "And I'm going to catch her killer."

"Yes, but it's been 48 hours already, and you've got nothing."

That was not the right thing to say. I realized that as his eyes narrowed at me, and he clenched his jaw. I had smashed an already exposed nerve. I bit my tongue. I wanted to kick myself.

"I'm aware of that," his voice deepened as he said that.

"I'm sorry, Drew. She's not the only one, and my dream is right on target even though you don't want to hear it."

I'd already made him mad. I figured I'd go all out now. I told him about Janice and Ken and handed him their card.

"You don't want to hear about the dream I had the other night, but I know there are other girls in danger."

"Not now, Grace."

"I can help you."

"I'm not fighting with you. Not here and not now."

"Fine, but my dream could help you, and you know it."

If only he'd listen to me.

"I'm taking this back to see if this will help any in the search. I'll come back when your flower orders are done."

At some point during this interlude, Emmie retreated into the workroom. I wasn't sure when. I watched an angry Drew leave the shop.

"Get this door bell fixed today. That's not a request," he said as he turned and walked out.

I left the front part of the shop to find Emmie. She was quick. She'd almost finished with a small "Get Well Soon" arrangement.

"You don't have to stay here."

51

"I know when I'm needed, and you need me but maybe as more of a friend than an employee."

I slumped into the chair in the room.

"True. I feel like I'm losing him, Emmie. We fight about stupid things."

As I said that, the tears came. I couldn't stop them this time.

Emmie put down her shears and walked over to me. She grabbed my hands.

"Drew loves you. I'm sure you'll work this out."

"What if I've already lost him?"

"He wouldn't still be with you. I lost one, remember? I know, and you haven't lost him. You're either overreacting or not telling me something."

"I hope you're right."

"I know I'm right. Drew still has a light in his eyes when he looks at you even when he's mad," she said. "He's got things to work through, but he will. I know he will. But the two of you have to talk about the root of your problem, and you know that."

I stood up and walked to the work table.

"He won't talk about his problems with me or anyone for that matter. He just keeps it all bottled up."

She gave me a weak smile.

"Emmie, could I ask a favor?"

"Of course."

"Would you draw another picture of the butterfly tattoo for me?"

Emmie nodded.

"Never give up, huh?"

"Never."

"Then, don't give up on Drew either."

6

The already cold trail kept getting colder for Drew over the next few days. The media's attention had turned from a dead Jane Doe to the city's preparations for the tournament and the festivities of the coming week. My internet searches for photos of the tattoo ran dry as well. It seemed this woman didn't exist. I didn't see Drew much. I'd gotten tired of going home to an empty house so I accepted my mother's invitation for a meal.

Soon after arriving I wondered if that had been such a good idea.

"I saw the lovely arrangement you made for Dana's baby," Mama said, right after giving me a hug and kiss on the cheek. "And Lily is beautiful."

Daddy was working on the crossword puzzle in the newspaper. I gave him a quick hug.

"Don't let her upset you," he whispered.

"I'll try, Daddy," I said and followed Mama into the kitchen.

"She has great genes, Mama. Of course, she's going to be beautiful. Mary Louise and Dana are gorgeous. Besides, Lily could look like a toad, and you'd still say she was beautiful."

That made my mother laugh.

"Well, she doesn't look like a toad. She's got beautiful skin and a ton of hair."

"It smells great in here."

I tried to change the conversation, but she didn't pay any attention to my comment.

"Mary Louise said you didn't deliver the flowers. She said Emmie did."

Mama busied herself in the kitchen and barely glanced at me when she said that. There was a roast in the oven, and several pots on the stove. I hadn't cooked in weeks. I mainly ate prepared salads or whatever was easy. A lot of times, I didn't even bother to eat.

"Yes, Emmie did because Drew took me out to celebrate his promotion on Friday. I told you about his promotion, remember?"

"I know, and I'm so excited for him."

"We had reservations at 6 so I left early."

"You still should have dropped it off to her. I know that wasn't the only one for her."

"Could we talk about something else?"

"Your brother will be visiting in a couple of weeks. He's going to be transferred to Fort Gordon soon so they are going to look for a house nearby."

"Really? Now, that is good news."

"Yes, they are going to need a big one. Sarah is expecting baby number four."

I felt like I'd been punched in the stomach.

"That's great. I hadn't heard that."

I tried to show a little enthusiasm at least, but I couldn't fake it.

"Well, Zack told me last night when he called. She's only a few weeks along."

I couldn't hold in the tears any longer.

"Could we please talk about something else?"

That came out harsher than I'd intended judging by the look on my mother's face when she turned around. She was pale as she walked to where I was seated and took me into her arms for a hug. I had tears streaming down my cheeks.

I knew my mother didn't mean anything by her baby comments. She wasn't trying to be insensitive, but sometimes, she got caught up in a moment. After all, she was going to be a grandmother again - no thanks to me, and Mary Louise became a grandmother for the first time after years of waiting for Hope Lily Andrews to arrive.

"I'm sorry," she said. "I didn't mean - "

"I know. Look, I hadn't told you this. I haven't really told anyone except for Drew, but I lost another baby a couple of months ago. Well about six months ago. Dana and I were due at the same time."

My mother stared at me. She'd knelt in front of the chair and released me from the bear hug.

"Oh, Grace. Why didn't you tell me?" she asked as she put her hand on my arm. I couldn't look at her in the eye.

"I couldn't bear the pain of another failure," I said, shaking my head.

"You're not a failure. This isn't your fault."

I couldn't stop the tears at this point. I tried to wipe them away. My mother grabbed a tissue.

"I kept it a secret. We were waiting until we were far enough along, but I'm glad now that we didn't say anything."

Conceiving was hard. Doctors blamed ovarian cysts and endometriosis as possible causes, but they weren't really sure what was wrong. I was otherwise healthy. When I did conceive, I had further problems, and I'd already miscarried four times. I was cautious and only told Drew. I was afraid to tell anyone at all. Emmie had guessed, and I hid it from my mother.

And Emmie was there when the last miscarriage happened. I was at the shop. She took care of me. I didn't want Drew to worry so I closed the shop, and Emmie came home with me while I called the doctor. She went with me to the follow up. People couldn't understand what I was going through, and I didn't want them to feel awkward around me. I'd already been through it before. People don't know what to say around someone who has lost a baby. They gave me empty platitudes that didn't ease the pain and often made matters worse. Some even said horrible things like "At least it happened before the baby was born." It was a cruel thing because I'd already envisioned a child when I saw the pregnancy test was positive. The babies were all very real to me.

Our marriage had already been strained, but the most recent miscarriage made the gulf even deeper. We'd always thought we'd have at least two or three children. Drew would make a great dad. He had a brother who lived in town. He and his wife had a couple of children. Drew was great with them. He was great when Emmie's kids and my brother's kids were around. It was so important to him. I felt like I'd let him down. I didn't have to tell him about the miscarriage; he could tell when he got home and found me curled up in bed with the lights off. He turned on the lights and pulled me close while I cried. I tried not to look at him, but I could see the pain and disappointment on top of everything else. My head told me that none of this was my fault, but there was part of me that wondered if I'd done something wrong. Even my doctor told me there was nothing I'd done to cause it. It was something they couldn't explain, and with each miscarriage, the glimmer of hope seemed to get smaller.

It was hard to be around Dana. She had no idea I'd been pregnant. At first I was thrilled because I could picture our babies growing up together just as she and I had done. I thought we'd get past the rough patch in our friendship. I was waiting to tell her after what I considered a safe point, but I never made it that far. With every one of her doctor's appointment and pregnancy milestones, the pain grew deeper. I wanted to be happy for her. I made to excuses to stay away from the gender reveal party and her baby shower. I stopped responding to her texts and answering calls, and I hid her on social media. I felt like an awful person for wanting those celebrations to be mine rather than hers. Yet, despite all the pain and uncertainty, there was still something inside that wanted to believe I'd be a mom.

"Oh, Grace. I just wish you'd told me."

"It hurt too much. I couldn't take everyone's looks of pity. I went back to the doctor last week. He doesn't have any good news. He doesn't think our chances of having a baby are good without some expensive medical intervention. Didn't Dana have in-vitro?"

"I still believe in miracles, honey. And doctors aren't always right. Lily is a miracle baby. Her parents tried for years to have a baby. They had some of the same struggles you did, and the doctors told them the same thing. I just thought maybe seeing them would give you some hope. Maybe Dana could help you? What about Beth's husband?"

"Beth's my friend, but I don't want her knowing so much about me. I know he's not supposed to talk about his patients. Beth's his wife, and she's highly persuasive. She would've made a great detective. She'd ask a lot of questions. I know her."

I took a breath.

"And I'm happy for Dana. Somewhere inside. I'm happy for her. Could we just not talk about babies tonight? I'm thinking about getting a dog, and I'm letting Emmie or Beth do all of the welcome baby and baby shower arrangements for a while. I just can't."

"How does Drew like his new job?"

"I haven't seen him much. He's working on a case. It's his first case, and he's really stressed out about it. He's afraid his first case will end up a cold case, but I'm not supposed to talk about that either. I can tell you that I have several parties I'm doing flowers for next week and that should help us through the slump we've had. At least, that's what I'm hoping."

"I made a lemon pound cake earlier today. Lemon pound cake makes everything better," my mother said as she patted my hand. "I think everything is almost ready."

My mother tried to make up for her actions the rest of the night. The meal with my parents turned out better than it started, and Mama was right about the lemon pound cake. It seemed to make things better. It always did.

I stayed as late as I could. I wanted to escape from sleep. I didn't know what the night held, and I was afraid to dream again. But several sleepless nights had gotten the best of me. I drifted off into a deep slumber almost as soon as I got into bed. Just when my body began to relax, the dreams came again. I walked through a building. It seemed to be a makeshift prison. Girls in cubicles, each with its own door and window looking in. I walked down the hallway, glancing into each cell. I saw women huddled alone in their cells, a simple cot for a bed. From the jerking motion of their shoulders, I could tell they were weeping. From there, they got up and dressed for the night, ready to be sold. They looked so young. I saw the same scenario as I passed each tiny cell. Each of them felt they had no choice, and some feared for their lives. I strained to see who was keeping them locked up. One of the young women turned and walked toward the door. She placed her hand on the small window and seemed to cry out for help. As I stood looking inside the room, I noticed my surroundings had changed. I hadn't left the building, but instead of it looking like the prison it was, it appeared to be a house. The stark room with a cot had turned into an exquisitely furnished home. I saw the hallway was covered with antique rugs; the walls were lined with fine works of art. I was confused as I pivoted to take in more of the building. I noticed there were windows in the hallway. Outside was a huge magnolia tree, towering over the house.

I sat up in bed and checked the clock. It was 3 a.m. I could feel my heart pounding in my chest. Drew had come home at one point and was sleeping beside me. I didn't want to wake him as I got out of bed. I understood what my dream meant. Even though the places the girls were staying were beautiful, they were still prisons. I found my dream journal where I'd written down so many dreams. I thought about Ken and Janice. I didn't know them well enough to tell them about the dreams I'd had. I sat in my overstuffed chair with my knees pulled close using them to balance my notebook as I wrote in it. Once finished, I sat motionless staring off into the darkness, wondering how I could help these women when Drew walked in.

"It's almost 4 o'clock," he said.

"I know."

He walked over and sat in a chair across from the couch.

"Why are you awake?"

58

"I don't sleep much these days, Drew. I try to avoid dreaming."

I didn't look at him when I said that. I heard him draw a deep breath.

"Neither do I," he said. I glanced up to see him seated on the couch. He was resting his elbows against his knees with his face buried in his hands.

"I know."

I wanted to tell him my dream. I was waiting for him to ask. Maybe that was me being stupid.

"Have you found anything on the wearer of the butterfly tattoo?" I whispered in the awkward silence.

"Nothing at all. I'm still trying to uncover leads, but I feel pressure to follow up on some other cases and let this one go. I feel like such a failure. My mom wants to have a party after the tournament, but I can't go there knowing I failed at my first case."

"You haven't failed, honey. You'll find the answers."

"I need to solve this, and we need to go on a vacation. I feel like I'm losing you, Grace."

I was surprised to hear him say that. I thought I was the only one who felt that way. I got up and moved to the couch where I sat in his lap.

"I'm not going anywhere, Drew. I love you no matter what."

He touched my face, running his fingertips across my cheekbone and pushing the hair out of my face.

"I believe in you, Drew."

"I don't know what I'd do if I lost you," he said as he kissed me. "We both need our sleep. It's going to be okay."

I nodded, and we headed back to bed. I fell back asleep, but he must've gotten dressed and left. I didn't sleep long. It was only 6:30, and I didn't open the shop until 9. It was going to be a busy day with tournament week looming in front of me. Emmie would be there to help, and Beth would do some of the behind-the-scenes work. I had a lot of paperwork on my desk. Orders to fill. I was there long before the 9 a.m. open on my sign.

I sat at my desk and stared at the second drawing of the tattoo that Emmie had created. I was deep in thought over my two dreams when I heard a voice from the front of the shop.

"Hello, Mrs. Ward?"

I heard a man's voice and walked out into the shop to see Ken and Janice. I brought a stack of papers out with me.

"Hi. I'm sorry. My door bell isn't working. I didn't hear you come in."

"That can be dangerous, you know, Mrs. Ward," Ken answered.

"My husband keeps telling me that. And please call me Grace."

I placed my papers on the counter.

"Your flowers should be in today. I have a few of them now, but I didn't think you wanted to start getting them until Sunday."

I was talking but neither of them were paying attention to me. They were looking at Emmie's drawing, and then Janice picked it up.

"What's wrong?"

"This drawing," Janice's voice broke as she said those two words. Her eyes never strayed from the paper.

"Oh, I didn't mean to bring that out here."

I didn't know what to say. I couldn't tell them what the drawing was.

"Who drew this?" Janice had tears forming in the corners of her eyes. She covered her mouth with her right hand as she held up the drawing with her left.

I bit my lip. They knew something. I knew none of this was a simple coincidence.

"Why do you ask?"

"It reminds us of someone we know," Ken whispered.

I could feel my heart racing, and I cleared my throat.

"I saw a young woman less than a week ago with this tattoo. Did you know her?"

Janice nodded slowly.

"We think her name was Amber. At least, that's what she told us."

I had to call Drew. He needed to meet this couple. They might have information on the case.

"Please, don't go anywhere. I need to call someone," I reached into my pocket for my cell phone and dialed Drew.

"Drew, you need to come to the shop. It's about the tattoo."

"What's going on?" asked Janice.

I paused. I wasn't really sure what I could tell them. We had to wait for Drew.

"My husband is a homicide investigator."

Janice gasped and turned to Ken. She buried her head in his chest and sobbed.

"I can't explain anything else until he arrives, but he's only a few minutes away."

Ken nodded.

Within minutes, Drew walked in the flower shop.

"Ken and Janice, this is my husband, Investigator Drew Ward."

"Baby, I need to use your office."

"Of course."

"You aren't open yet so would you lock the door? Please call and see about getting your door bell fixed today."

He looked directly at me when he said that. I'd gotten so busy that it had slipped my mind again. I nodded. My office wasn't large. There was my chair at the desk and another chair across from it. Janice sat in the chair and Ken stood behind her.

"This is Ken and Janice from that organization I told you about. Or at least I think I did. They may know something about the tattoo."

Drew nodded and looked at the couple. He had a folder and in it was a police photograph of the woman's body after it had been pulled from the Savannah River.

"I need to show you something that will be disturbing," he said to Janice.

She nodded.

"Do you know this woman?"

61

Janice began crying more. Ken nodded.

"She said her name was Amber, but we don't think it was. Several teams talked to her. She didn't want to be out on the streets, but she was afraid. We weren't sure if she was afraid of her pimp or what. She said she was 19."

Ken shook his head and paused for a moment.

"We don't think she was that old," he continued. "We think she was probably underage and a runaway. Maybe that's what she was afraid of. She might have thought that we'd send her back into a bad family or the foster care system if we knew her real age and real name. But we don't think that she was from Georgia. Her accent was different. She had a definite Cajun twang. We talked about college football one time, and she said something about Louisiana State. People tend to go for the home team in college football."

"The last time we saw her was about 10 days ago. She called us and asked one of the teams to meet her. She wanted us to help her," Janice words were choppy as she spoke through her tears.

"She didn't show up at the meeting site," said Ken. "The team waited for more than an hour."

"We found her body a week ago. What about the tattoo?" Drew asked. "It must've been expensive. It was a work of art."

"We first met her about a year ago. She didn't have it then. A few months ago, she had it. We commented on it because it was beautiful. It was definitely a work of art. She never told us about it, but one of the other team members said she told them that it was for her sister. She died when she was 10. She had leukemia," said Janice.

"Is there anyone from your team who might could help us get some more information on her?"

"We can ask. She worked the same part of Atlanta. You know, people come to Atlanta because there are so many movie and TV shows being filmed there now. It's like Hollywood. People come with big dreams, and people prey on those dreams. Some of the pimps say they can get them modeling contracts, and they get the girls hooked on drugs. It's not pretty," Ken said.

"What happened to Amber?" Janice asked.

"We're waiting on the autopsy and toxicology reports. Do you know who might have been trafficking her? Why are you here? Why this week?"

"Sex is big business," said Ken. "It always has been, and this golf tournament brings in a lot of men with money to spend. Girls are brought here from several cities, not just Atlanta. I'm sure they don't wait until the week of the tournament to just show up. Whoever it was may have brought Amber down to give potential buyers a sample of the goods."

"Stop talking that way, Ken," Janice snapped.

"You know that's how they treat those girls," he replied.

"I know that, but I can't stand to hear it put that way," she said, wiping a few tears away.

"Where do you think they are going to be this week?" Drew asked.

"Do you really want to know?"

"Yes, I do."

"Check behind those walls of those gated communities. There's probably one house with a bunch of beautiful young women. Whoever is selling these girls won't do it in seedy part of town. They want top dollar for their merchandise, and they have to present a picture of grace and class."

I gasped. I didn't realize I'd made any noise until Drew turned his head to glance at me. I shook my head at him, but my dream made so much sense now.

"What else do you know?"

"My guess is that there's a fresh batch of girls. They know that rich and famous people come here for this golfing event. They've probably been told they have to come here to meet some of them to get a contract or get noticed. There are international connections here for the week. I think they brought Amber along because they knew they were getting ready to lose her. Judging by that tattoo, she turned a huge profit for them."

"Do you have any idea where she got the tattoo?"

"No clue. There are a lot of tattoo places in Atlanta."

"It was strange we couldn't find any photos of it. No one proud to show off that piece."

"Amber was secretive about things. She seemed like a sweet girl who got mixed up in the wrong crowd."

"So help me a little more. You said she was trying to get away. They kill and dump her here to throw off the scent of their Atlanta operation?" Drew speculated out loud. "We saw her with a man - 50s, dark hair, scar on his cheek, and a New York accent."

"Atlanta is a melting pot for all types. He's probably not an important member of the group. He doesn't ring any bells. He's just a flunky."

"But this flunky could be a murderer."

"Maybe, but if he was a handler, killing her wasn't a wise move. If he damaged the merchandise, he could be in a lot of trouble from the higher-ups. You might be looking for a second body, but I doubt you'll find it."

Drew glanced at Janice then at Ken.

"Do you have anyone else here who might've come in contact with Amber or do you know how I can find people who might know her?"

Ken nodded.

"Yes, there are a couple of people who might know some more, but they're in Atlanta."

"Who?"

"We know that she lived with a couple of other girls. These girls all probably worked for the same guy. We've tried to help them all, but they are scared."

Drew nodded.

"Listen, I've got a few friends on the force in Atlanta, and there are people with our organization who might be able to help you as well. I have some numbers in my phone, but I need to call someone for the rest," said Ken.

"That would be great," said Drew.

"Janice, I'm going to the car for a minute."

When Ken and Drew slipped out of the office, I moved closer to Janice.

"It doesn't sound like you knew Amber well."

"Maybe not, but if you forget these girls and sometimes young men are people with real names, real families, real lives, then you're no good to them. You have to have compassion for them. Some have made really bad choices, but others got sucked into a world they didn't know existed and can't get out. It's easy for people to get calloused and want to toss them away. Amber seemed to be such a sweet girl. And at the end, I think she wanted to try to have a life."

"Why did you have that sketch?" Janice asked.

"I - "

Drew came back into the room interrupting my sentence.

"Babe, I've got a lot of phone calls to make, or I may just need to make a trip up to Atlanta," he paused and gazed into my eyes. "Thank you."

Drew gave me a quick kiss and rushed to the door. As he opened it, he turned.

"Get your doorbell fixed - today."

"Yes. I will do that."

I turned to Ken.

"The truck with your flowers should be here around 11," I said, glancing at the clock. They'd come in early. It wasn't even 9 yet. "I can call you when they are in."

"Thank you."

"I don't mean to be rude," Janice began. "How did you have that drawing?"

"I'm not sure what I'm supposed to say. My husband and I went to dinner last Friday to celebrate his promotion to detective, and on our way into the restaurant, I saw Amber in the parking lot. She was talking to an older man. He was holding her wrist, and I could see the tattoo. My husband spoke to them. The man was rude. They raced off out of the parking lot. The next morning I had a wedding downtown that I had to deliver flowers to. While we were there decorating the venue, I heard some loud screams. When I went to investigate, I saw Amber's body face up in the Savannah River tangled in a net or vines or a net or something. I had to give a statement about the previous night, and we've been looking for this tattoo ever since."

"How did she die? I know your husband said they were still waiting on the autopsy."

"They are. Drew told me she was shot, but I don't know if that's the cause of death."

I didn't want to tell Janice about what else had been done to Amber's body, and I figured I'd leave out the part about the dreams I had.

"Had she ever been arrested?" I asked.

"Not to my knowledge. "

I nodded.

"I told your husband a couple of places where we might be giving out flowers. It could give him a lead although I know these criminals are hoping the police will be distracted by the tournament and all the visitors and will look the other way," Ken said.

"I'm so glad you just happened into my shop."

"I don't believe in coincidences," said Janice. "I think that things happen for a reason. And we were definitely supposed to meet you. Maybe with your husband's help, this one group will be shut down."

"I believe the same way."

It wasn't long before Emmie arrived, and I couldn't wait to share the news with her about the tattoo. Around 10:30, the van delivering our order showed up. I was more concerned with getting the flowers in than I was with looking around, but a flash of light caught my eye. It must have been the sun hitting the chrome mirror on the vehicle across the street. I looked at it and noticed a man standing next to a sports car. I tried to breathe. I felt like the air had been sucked out of my lungs. I had to get into the shop without looking like I was running.

Inside, I lingered. I hated letting Emmie bring the flowers in, but I couldn't. I tried to take a deep breath. Was it just a coincidence? He couldn't have remembered me from that night at the restaurant. I'm sure I didn't make that much of an impact. Maybe it wasn't even him, and how could he have tracked me down at my shop. My imagination was getting the best of me.

Within a few minutes, Emmie had walked in.

"What's wrong, sweetie? You're as pale as a ghost."

"The man across the street," I choked the words out.

Emmie looked outside.

"What man?"

"Dark hair, gray streaks, sports car. He was smoking a cigarette."

"I don't see anyone."

I walked to the window and stared, but he was gone. Was my mind playing tricks on me?

"What's the matter?"

"But he was just there. It was the man I saw with Amber that night."

"Are you sure?"

"Emmie, all I've done for the past week is see that girl, that man, that tattoo."

"Maybe it's just a coincidence."

"You know I don't believe in those."

"Plus, I had another dream last night, and then Ken tells Drew exactly what I saw in my dream."

"You have to tell Drew about your dreams."

"He won't listen."

"Make him, sweetie. You have to make him. It's not your fault that you tried to warn him about something, and he didn't listen. You'd think after he found the body he'd listen to you."

"If Drew is anything, he's stubborn. He decided he doesn't want to hear my dreams, and he's not going to let his pride get in the way no matter how on-target they are."

I needed to work. I grabbed some flowers and began working on one of the "Get Well Soon" arrangements that I had been called in. Maybe I was seeing things now.

"Emmie, would you call someone to get the doorbell fixed?"

"Sure."

I tried calling Drew's cell phone several times, but he wasn't answering. Maybe he couldn't. In between phone calls, I felt drawn to look out the window. Was the man there? Did he see me? Did he remember me?

Finally, my phone rang.

"Drew, I saw him," I didn't wait for him to say anything before I blurted everything out. "I saw the man with Amber. He was in front of the coffee shop across the street. I know it was him."

"Babe, I'm in Atlanta. I'm meeting with a couple of people here. I've got a few leads. I'm coming back, but it may be tomorrow."

"I'm scared, Drew."

"I'll have someone drive by. Do you have your gun with you?"

"You know I hate that thing."

"I don't care how you feel about it. I've taught you how to use it to protect yourself, and I want to know you are safe even if I can't be there with you."

"Yes, I have it in my purse."

"Put it on you where you can get to it quickly," he paused. "And you're sure that it was the same man?"

"Yes, Drew. I'm positive."

"Keep your eyes open, and if you see anything else, call me immediately. Are you alone?"

"No, Emmie is here."

"Try to keep someone in there with you, and I'll have someone come by to check on you as well."

"Okay."

Emmie had called to have the door chime looked at, but no one was available the Friday before the golf tournament. I tried not to panic. I had two big parties Sunday night and then there were private functions non-stop for the next week. I considered locking the door, but I didn't want to deter any business. In the front portion of my shop were several cases with simple floral arrangements, plus some loose stems for any walk-in business. Also there was a selection of stuffed animals, balloons, and other gifts. There was a window from the work room into the storefront so I could keep an eye out for walk-ins. But Drew was right. I really needed to get the doorbell fixed. I often got so engrossed in the flowers that I didn't watch for people to come in, and I didn't hear them either.

I tried to put my mind on something else. Emmie had gone into the back storeroom to get some greenery, and she startled me when she returned.

"Hey, it's just me," she said as she put a bucket on the work table.

"I'm sorry."

"I saw a police car just a few minutes ago."

"I know. My mind is going crazy."

"If we stay focused, we can finish these and get out of here," Emmie said.

"What if this man knows where I live? Or where you live?"

"Sweetie, just calm down. You're married to a cop, and he will take care of you. I'm positive."

"But he's not here right now, is he?"

"No, but he's got someone watching out for you."

"Hey, Grace. She's right. Drew is looking out for you," a deep voice called out, startling me once again. I looked up to see Butch. "And so am I."

"Hi, Butch. Thank you for stopping in."

"It's no problem. Are you okay?"

"A little shaken and jumpy, but otherwise, yeah, I'm fine."

"How about you, Emmie?" he asked.

"I'm not the one you need to be concerned about," she smiled at him.

"I'll be driving by and looking out for you. I haven't seen the car with that plate though," he said.

I nodded. I was beginning to think I'd imagined it.

"Have a good day and you too, Emmie," he said and left the shop.

"See, Drew loves you," Emmie said.

"I know. Emmie, do you think I could stay with you again tonight? Drew won't be at home. He's in Atlanta. I liked our girls' night Saturday. Maybe we can have another one tonight."

"Of course, you can stay with me. I think that's a good idea."What kind of ice cream should we get?" Emmie asked.

"I had way too much ice cream last week. We should try something less fattening."

"Well, that's no fun."

"Emmie, you have never battled the bulge. Even when you were pregnant, you barely gained any weight. People asked me after your babies were born if you and Blake adopted because they didn't believe you were ever pregnant."

Emmie chuckled.

"How about smoothies then? We can make them out of bananas, strawberries, blueberries and some almond milk."

"Sure. That sounds fine."

"And comedies. Lots of comedies."

7

I stayed at Emmie's until midnight. Drew called and said he would be heading home late. I didn't really want to go home alone, but I wanted to see Drew. Of course, he wasn't there when I got home, but I was a little paranoid from his constant asking about the doorbell at my shop. I took out my gun and did my best impression of clearing the room from all the spy movies I'd seen. I was relieved that no one had broken in, and I rechecked all the locks in the house. I tried to wait up for Drew, but I must've dozed off. I heard sounds in the living room and noticed it was 1 a.m. I took my gun with me, not that I thought I could ever really shoot anyone. Drew was standing in the dark near the desk where he had the liquor. He was pouring himself a drink when I came in. As the moonlight shimmered off the liquid, I could tell the bottle was close to being empty.

"Please don't do that," the words came out before I realized it.

"It's a crime for a man to have a drink in his own house?" his voice dripped with sarcasm as he turned and looked at me with his hands raised. It wasn't just sarcasm I heard. He sounded angry with me.

"I'm sorry."

As I put the gun down, Drew dropped his arms.

"If you could stop at 'a drink,' I might not have a problem with it."

Talking when you are on edge and still half-asleep is not a good

71

idea. At least it's not for me. Sometimes things come out that you might not have said under other circumstances, and those words came out harsher than I anticipated. He didn't realize what his sudden addiction to alcohol was doing to us. Maybe it wasn't the alcohol itself. The alcohol was just a symptom of underlying problems and our inability to deal with them or even talk about them for that matter. I was tired of walking on eggshells, wondering if I was going to say the wrong thing at the wrong time. I noticed his jaw tighten. His eyes narrowed drilling holes into my soul. I could feel my heart pounding.

" Until a few months ago, you never drank at all, Drew."

"Things change. People change," he said as he picked up the glass and threw the contents down his throat. He started to pour another, but I walked over to him and covered the glass. Lack of sleep was making me bold. I was afraid to look at him so I kept my eyes on my hand. I knew he was already angry. He'd never done anything to hurt me so I'm not sure where the fear came from. I wasn't sure what I was expecting to happen next. He put down the bottle, and he covered my hand. He moved close to me. I could feel his breath on my cheek and could smell the alcohol. I turned to gaze into his eyes. It might have been dark in the room, but I could see. What I saw didn't frighten me. Instead, I felt his pain, and my fear melted. I could see the demons he was battling, the grief, the fear, the anger, the helplessness, all the things he wanted to drown and make go away. I knew exactly what he was feeling. I'd felt it too. I was guilty, but instead of drinking to forget, I think I drowned my pain in flowers and trying to build a business instead of running into his arms. We were both guilty of holding things in and not dealing with them. He broke my gaze and looked at the bottle. He stared at it and shook his head. I wondered what he was thinking.

"I'm not out here to pick a fight with you, Drew."

I turned and reached out to touch his face.

"I'm on your side, remember? Vows, church, for better, for worse, you and I are a team. I made that promise 10 years ago, and I don't intend to break it."

He didn't respond immediately.

The physical part of our relationship hadn't completely died, but it had been only that for months - physical, mechanical. It served a purpose. For me, that purpose was to conceive a baby, but there was little intimacy as both of us put up our walls. I'd hoped when I saw the romantic Drew on the night of the murder that things were changing. Maybe they had. He covered my hand with his and pulled it to his lips. He kissed my palm and looked into my eyes. I saw a tenderness in his eyes that I hadn't seen in months. I'll never forget that look. It always caused me to melt.

"I love you, Drew, but I can't stand back and watch you kill yourself."

"I love you too, Grace," he said as he pulled me close. He held me tightly then stepped back. He looked at me and brushed my face with the tips of his fingers. He tilted my chin with his finger and kissed me. The first kisses were gentle, but all of his emotions and my emotions seemed to rush to the surface all at once.

"I don't want to talk anymore," he whispered into my ear as he began to kiss my neck.

Neither did I.

I was surprised when I woke up before him the next morning. Usually he was awake and gone well before sunrise. I watched him sleep. He seemed so peaceful. I knew he had a busy day before him, and so did I. Since Emmie and I hadn't binged on ice cream the night before, I was hungry. I could at least make breakfast before we had to go our separate ways.

I was putting on some coffee when he came into the kitchen. It was mainly for him since I didn't care for the stuff. He walked up behind me and kissed the back of my neck.

"I'm going to need lots of that," he said.

"Coffee or kissing?" I asked as I turned around and linked my arms around his neck.

He smiled.

"If I didn't have a murder investigation, I'd say kissing."

"I think you need that anyway."

"You're probably right, but I do have to go soon."

His smile faded. He was right about needing that coffee. He had bags and dark circles under his eyes.

"The coffee will be ready shortly. You should've stayed in bed I would've brought it to you. "

"Then, I never would make it into work."

"I take it your trip to Atlanta didn't end well?"

He sat down at the kitchen table and ran his hands through his hair.

"More questions than answers. It seems every question opens up more questions, and every answer brings with it more questions. I talked to some of the other people in Ken and Janice's organization. They remembered Amber, but they couldn't tell me anything else except that it wasn't her real name which could have been Michelle or Christy. She'd never been arrested. There are no records of her. I talked to some of the police up there, but they didn't have anything. We went out and tried to talk to some of the prostitutes who might have known her, but of course, they didn't trust us, not that I expected them to."

I sat down next to him as the coffee continued to brew.

"Maybe, I could go out with Janice and Ken. Someone they reach out to might know who this person was or who killed her."

He shook his head.

"Absolutely not. I 'm not putting you in danger."

"How would that be putting me in danger?"

"Tell me about the man outside your shop. Did you see him again after you called me?"

"No, I kept checking outside, and Emmie never saw him. You don't think it's a coincidence, do you?"

"Did you see a police car?"

"Yes, we did, and Butch even came in and checked on us."

Drew smiled.

"Did you know that Butch likes Emmie, but he's too afraid to ask her out?"

"Really? I didn't know they knew each other very well."

"He met her at Christmas several years ago. She was still married at the time so she probably doesn't remember, but he does. And of course, they've both been to our 4th of July cookouts and a few other things here."

I smiled. I could see that now. I thought I saw him looking more at her than me when he came in.

"He seems like a nice guy, and he did seem more concerned with her than me."

"Did Butch see anyone?"

"I don't think so. If he did, he didn't say anything. Maybe he wanted us to feel safe."

"I'm not trying to doubt you, but are you sure it was the same guy? He's taking some big risks especially coming out in that car with that vanity plate. That's something people will notice."

"Yes, I'm positive it was him."

"Did you get your doorbell fixed?"

"Emmie called, but they couldn't come out yesterday. They said it would be Monday."

"Then buy some bells or something to put on your door, and don't forget to take this with you," he said as he placed my gun on the table and slid it to me. "I'm glad to see you had it with you last night when I got home, and I'm glad you didn't shoot me."

At least, he laughed when he said that.

The gun. I hated that thing. Maybe it wasn't the gun I hated as much as the fact that my husband felt I needed to have it with me at all times because nowhere was safe.

"Why are you acting this way?" My heart was pounding. I knew what he was going to say that this man knew who I was and that I could link him to the body in the river, and that's why my city wasn't safe for me.

He reached out and touched my hand as I stared at the gun. I held my breath as he started to talk.

"You and I are alike in a lot of ways. You and I can sense when things aren't right. We call it different things. And my gut is telling me that something isn't right here besides the obvious."

"If we're so much alike, then why won't you listen to my dreams? Your hunches aren't proof of anything."

"It's not the same thing."

"You just said it was. Make up your mind, Drew. You know that we're alike, but you refuse to listen to me."

He clenched his jaw and narrowed his eyes as he stared at me. He ignored my comments.

"We're just going through a rough time. We'll get through this, Grace. When we get through this week and this case, I'm going to take some vacation time, and you and I will go somewhere. "

I tried not to get angry with him. I hated confrontation. I hated fighting. I believed in keeping the peace even if that meant I was the one taking the punishment, but not this time, not today. I'd held it in last night, but for some reason, I couldn't hold it in any longer. I'm not sure what he said that pushed me over the edge. Maybe it had been building in me. It certainly came to the surface the night before, but once again, I pushed it back under.

"You keep saying that, Drew, but if you don't get help for you, what good will it do for us to go away and come back the same?"

He leaned back in his chair. He folded his arms across his bare chest and tilted his head at me.

"I'm fine, Grace, just fine. I passed all of those psychological tests after I came back from my leave, and I got a promotion. The sheriff's department thinks I'm fine too."

"That's because you know all the right things to say to pass those things. You aren't stupid. You knew what they wanted to hear even if it wasn't the truth. You weren't about to lose your job, and I get that."

"Where exactly is this going, Grace?" his tone dropped with that question, and his eyes narrowed at me. He leaned forward at the table. He was trying to make me back down, and I'd been backing down from him for months. And in that time, I'd seen my husband spiral into someone I didn't know. I'd never been afraid of Drew. He'd never been violent toward me, and I rarely saw him angry. But I never challenged him either. Until this point, the only arguments we had were over whether to order Chinese or Mexican for dinner. We always got along. But he was right, things and people change. As I stared at him, there was something I didn't like. It was almost like he was daring me. Daring me to what? Stand up to him? Did he want to upset me? Did he want to see me angry? Maybe he needed to.

"You have to face what happened. You need to talk to someone who understands. Drowning your emotions in alcohol isn't helping you," I lowered my voice. I tried not to get emotional. I wanted to sound rational despite the fact that the hair on the back of my neck was bristling, and I wanted to spit nails I was so angry.

"And who can understand it, Grace? Your pastor? Has he ever killed anyone? Has he ever been there when his best friend killed his wife, and nothing he could do or say would stop it?"

Mark and Linda. It was that day. The day everything changed.

There was an edge to that sentence as he emphasized the "your." I felt like I'd been punched in the stomach.

"No, but that's not the point. Pastor B used to be your pastor too," I had a hard time getting those words out as I struggled to breathe.

"Maybe, but not anymore."

"Why, Drew? Faith has always been a huge part of your life and our life together. I don't understand."

That apparently was the tipping point. The tone of Drew's voice dropped again, but each sentence seemed to get louder as his jaw hardened.

"Where was God on that day, Grace ? Where was He? Where was He on the day you miscarried again? And where is He now?" Drew raised his voice with each question, and he stood up.

"He's here. He always has been."

This wasn't going well. I didn't expect it would, but he had to face what had been happening in our lives. Our problems weren't going to vanish. He had to confront his problem - our problem. Maybe this had to happen. I just wish it hadn't happened this way with angry words.

"Oh, really? If He was here and He really loved us as you say He does, then why don't we have any children? Why can't you have a baby? If you have all these dreams for other people, why hasn't your dream about us happened?"

His voice continued to rise. This is not where I thought it would go. I was talking about something completely different, but the force of his words went straight through my heart. It hurt worse than him hitting me with his fist. I took a deep breath. Of course, I'd asked myself the same questions. I was mad at God; I was mad at myself. I was even mad at Drew. We'd been married for 10 years. I wasn't getting any younger. At the heart of this discussion was my own sense of inadequacy. I was the reason we couldn't have children. It wasn't him. It was me, but there was a sliver of hope.

"Dana Andrews had a baby despite all the doctors' tests and reports that she'd never have one. I'll have a baby one day, Drew. It's my faith that will bring me through this. It used to be our faith that bonded us and kept us together. And you can discount my dreams all you want, but I know they are true and so do you. Those dreams I've had of holding a baby girl are what keep me going. And I've had more than one dream of a baby. Now, I'm seeing my dreams happen almost as soon as I have them. They confirm to me that it will happen. It's a question of when not if for me, Drew. And you should listen to me about them because they could help your case."

I could feel the tears streaming down my face as I practically yelled the words at him. So much for not getting emotional. I'd kept all of this in for too long. There wasn't anything to hold me back now. I didn't care. I couldn't deal with the emotions any more. I knew I'd been on the verge of exploding so I exploded.

Drew stood up and took a step closer to me so I stood up and took a breath because I wasn't done. Now was my chance to tell him what I hadn't been able to in months, what had been building up. I'd never seen that expression on his face. It was a strange mix of shock and anger.

"And I can't do anything about the day Mark and Linda died. That's what I was talking about, not the whole baby thing. You've got to stop reliving it and punishing yourself for it. It wasn't your fault. There was nothing you could have done to change the outcome. You and I both know that. Go ahead. Blame God. Yell at Him. He tried to warn you, but you didn't listen then either. You didn't listen to my dreams then. They warned us, and you almost died that day too because you didn't listen. So, yell at me. Hate me for what I'm saying to you even though you know I'm telling you the truth. Do what you need to do, but get over your anger before it destroys you. You don't think I know how much you are drinking. Well I don't exactly, but I know it's a lot and I know it's often, and if you keep that up, you will kill yourself. I love you too much to watch you do this to yourself. And you know what else? At this moment, I'm thankful I haven't had a baby with you because of what you are doing to yourself and us. I can't take this anymore. I'm probably going to stay at Emmie's this week. You won't be here much anyway so you won't notice."

I rushed out of the kitchen for our bedroom because I couldn't hold back the tears any longer. My hands were shaking, and I couldn't breathe. I could hear Drew cursing and the sounds of glass shattering against the floor. I think it was my coffee pot. It didn't matter. I couldn't stay in the house any longer. I wasn't sure where I'd go. I threw on some clothes. I didn't really care what I looked like and headed out the front door. As I passed the kitchen, I saw the broken coffee pot and coffee puddle on the floor, and Drew sitting at the kitchen table with his hands covering his face. I hoped he was thinking about what I'd said, but I couldn't talk to him anymore. I was getting angrier by the minute, and I knew I'd already said enough. I guess he heard the front door. As I reached my car, I heard him calling my name. I didn't look up. I got in and drove off.

The sun had come up, but it was still too early to open the shop. I didn't know where to go. I didn't want to bother Emmie, but she'd know what happened soon enough. I drove to a shopping center parking lot, where I sat in my car and cried. For some reason, Ken and Janice popped into my head. I understood Drew's reasoning when he said he didn't want me to go out with them, but I wanted to help. I wanted to do something good with my life. I wanted it to matter.

I had Ken's card with his cell number in my purse. I pulled it out and stared at it. I called it and was surprised when he answered.

"Hi, Ken, this is Grace Ward. I was wondering if I could talk to you and Janice."

He gave me the address of where they were staying. It wasn't far from the shopping center, and I was there within a few minutes.

"Good morning."

"Are you okay?" asked Janice.

"It's complicated."

"Come in and have some coffee. Have you had breakfast? I've made grits and eggs."

"I didn't mean to interrupt."

"You haven't interrupted a thing. We love having people around."

I felt awkward stopping by and disturbing their breakfast. I was still rattled from my argument with Drew so I blurted out a reason for my visit.

"I want to help you and your organization."

"You are already helping us with the flowers," Ken said.

"But there must be something more. I want to see justice for Amber. My husband didn't get much from his trip to Atlanta. Maybe they'd talk to me. I don't know. I want to go with you."

"We aren't just going after the girls being brought in from Atlanta. We also have groups that are going to help with the problem here. "

"I feel so helpless."

"Grace, this may sound strange, but we feel that you know more than you are telling us."

That was an odd remark, and I know my shocked expression gave me away.

"You will probably think I'm crazy."

"We've met some crazy people, strung out on drugs and doing crazy things. You've struck us as pretty normal," said Ken.

"On the night Amber was killed, I had a dream about it so when I discovered her body..." I couldn't finish the sentence. The image of her body was something I couldn't shake. I'd been so grateful that her eyes were closed.

Janice smiled.

"That doesn't sound strange at all," she replied.

"Really?"

Janice shook her head.

"Really."

I told her about my other dreams. I think I'd been having one a night despite the fact that I barely had any sleep. They were similar, but there were different details in each one of them.

I'd also had another dream that I hadn't even told Emmie about. In that one, I was in danger. I was trying to help a girl like Amber and found myself staring down the barrel of a gun. I wasn't sure how that dream ended. I woke up before it finished.

I'd done a good job keeping the raw emotion back or so I thought, but I couldn't help it any more. Tears began to flow down my cheeks as I recounted the dreams and Drew's reactions to them. They'd asked how Drew felt so I told them.

"I'm sorry. I need to go."

Janice walked over to me and gave me a big hug. I felt like a blubbering idiot standing there in the kitchen, hugging a woman a barely knew and telling her my life story.

"I can't believe I'm telling complete strangers all of my problems."

"That's what happens when you bottle things up," said Janice.

"Thank you. I didn't mean to burden you with all of this."
Janice smiled.

"I told you that I believed we met for a reason. Sometimes that reason isn't always what we think it is."

I nodded.

"I'm sorry. I have to get to my shop. Thank you for everything, and if there's any other way I can help you, please let me know."

I was glad I hadn't put on any makeup before I left because it would've been gone by now anyway. I had makeup at the shop. I kept it for times like these. Maybe I could hide the damage before Emmie got there, but she could've been a detective with her eye for detail. She didn't miss anything. I was early so I rushed into the bathroom to put on my mask. When I came out, I saw a woman standing in the store.

"I'm sorry my doorbell isn't working. I hope you haven't been waiting long."

"Oh no, hon, I just walked in. I'm hoping you can help me," the woman said in a Southern accent sweeter than iced tea on a summer's afternoon. She looked and smelled like she'd been dipped in a vat of roses. Her hair, nails, and makeup were perfect; everything matched the dominant pink in her floral patterned dress.

"I can try. What exactly do you need?"

"Well, hon, I'm Claire. My husband and I are in town from Charleston for the tournament next week. We've rented this lovely house on Walton Way, and I am serving as the hostess at the parties for his corporate partners. We will have several functions on the lanai and the grounds this week. I got so caught up in the planning I forgot to confirm my order with my regular florist. I'm beside myself because he is booked solid this week. Flowers are just not something I'm going to have the time to fiddle with, and I need some stunning centerpieces for my tables. Everything has to be perfect. This could mean a promotion for my husband."

"I understand. Here are a few designs that might work well for your party," I pulled out a portfolio with some of my photographs to give Claire an idea of what I could provide plus pricing.

"Oh, these are incredible," she said as she flipped through the designs. "Yes, I've definitely come to the right place."

"How did you find me?"

"Internet, but I needed to meet you first, hon," she said. She looked up briefly and gave me a broad smile. She pointed to several pricey arrangements. "I want these. Can you get them to me Tuesday? Here's the address."

She slid me a piece of paper and her platinum credit card.

"I need them around 3 o'clock. If you have any trouble, call me."

Claire left in a mist of her strong floral perfume. As I glanced at the order she'd placed, I thought I might have to sit down for a few minutes. Emmie was definitely getting that bonus. This was the largest order I'd had in months. It was even better than Jimmy Hughes.

"Good Saturday morning to you," Emmie said.

She was practically standing over me. I didn't hear her come in. I was still stunned.

"Yes, it's going to be a great morning."

Emmie tilted her head at me and stared for a second.

"Well, you're smiling, but your eyes are puffy."

"And that means what?" I looked away, trying to avoid Emmie's stare, but I knew it was pointless. She was like a hunting dog honed in on its prey.

"That something good just happened to make you forget all the crying you did before it."

"You're in the wrong business. You should become a detective."

"I'm your best friend, remember?"

Emmie followed as we went to my computer. I had to make a quick order for these wholesale flowers, and I couldn't look her in the eye.

"We got a huge order for next week. Something in addition to everything else. I'm going to be able to give you a huge bonus

83

this month, Emmie. Someone came in and ordered several of your designs. Remember the Finch wedding from last year? And the Goldberg wedding?"

Emmie had a big grin on her face.

"She loved those. She ordered several just like them for three different parties. "

"I loved those too. I was feeling super creative that day."

Her smile faded with her next sentence.

"Why are your eyes still puffy?"

"I don't want to talk about it."

"Didn't we just go over this whole best friend thing?"

"I know."

"Best friends don't keep anything from each other."

I couldn't t look at Emmie. I thought I might start crying again.

"Drew and I had a huge fight this morning. I've kept my mouth shut for so long, tried to be that good wife everyone says I'm supposed to be, but I couldn't do it any longer."

"What happened?" she asked as she sat down across from me.

"He said he wanted to go away after the tournament and after he solves his first case, and I snapped. I let him have it. What good will it do if he doesn't come face to face with what's bothering him? So I've spent most of the morning crying. And I may need a place to stay."

I didn't look at her until I said that last part about needing a place to stay.

I couldn't hold back the tears any longer. Emmie came over and gave me a hug. After a few minutes, she disappeared, but quickly returned with an entire roll of toilet paper.

"Really?"

I giggled a minute through the tears. I didn't think I was going to cry that much.

"Take what you need," she said blandly.

"I haven't said anything about this, but Drew's been drinking a lot lately. He tries to hide some of it from me. He usually drinks late at night."

"Drew drinking? Are you serious? I've never seen Drew drink anything other than sweet tea."

"He started right after Mark and Linda died. Then I miscarried right after that. Too much happened at one time. He doesn't think that I know how much he's drinking. And I don't really. I know it's a lot for him and it's getting worse. He's stopped hiding it from me. He needs to talk to someone other than me. When he's talking to me these days, he's not saying anything. It's empty. I can't make it right."

"I'll say an extra prayer for you today, Grace."

"Thanks. Let's get to work."

"I've got some arrangements to make."

I nodded. I had way too much to do this morning. Golf tournament week also meant something else; tax day was on its heels. The golf tournament is held annually the first full week of April. I had a lot of paperwork to get together. It was so complicated that it made my head swim. I'd brought in our personal paperwork as well. I usually didn't wait until the last minute, but this year, the date slipped up on me. I'd kept up with the quarterly stuff, but our personal stuff wasn't as organized as it usually was. The miscarriage and Drew's problems had sent me into a spin in so many ways. Thankfully, my accountant doesn't care for golf.

I got lost in receipts, and I had no idea what time it was. As I was flipping through some files, I was startled as a hand reached from behind me holding a small box with a pink bow on top of it. I knew exactly where that box had come from and who was putting it on my desk. I didn't know if I could look at Drew or not at this point. I was still upset rattled from this morning.

"A man usually apologizes with flowers, but since you own a flower shop, I thought that might put me in even more hot water if I got flowers from someone else," he whispered in my ear.

I thought about Jimmy Hughes, and I couldn't help but smile at that.

I turned around to see him on his knees next to me.

"Sweets for the sweet," he said. The box was marked with the Cupcakery's logo. The shop was located around the corner. They had the best chocolate peanut butter cheesecake cupcake. I stared at the box. I knew that was exactly what was inside it. I think the road to my heart was paved with chocolate and cheesecake, and Drew knew it.

"Thanks, Drew."

"Is that a smile somewhere I see?"

He lifted an eyebrow at me and gave me a hopeful smile.

"Do you mind if I sit down?"

"Go ahead."

He closed the door behind him before sitting down.

"You're right about some of the things you said this morning," he said.

I didn't know what to say. I only nodded.

"After you left and I cleaned up the coffee almost cutting myself on the pieces of glass, I got dressed and drove around. I've been thinking about what you said all morning. Grace, you know me better than I know myself. You've always been there for me, and I'm sorry that I've hurt you this morning and for the past several months. It didn't take a rocket scientist to figure out that all I've been through is hurting you when I was only trying to drown my pain. I know you were hurting to begin with. I know how much having a baby means to you, and I haven't been there for you when you've tried to be there for me. Grace, hurting you is the last thing I've ever wanted to do."

He moved around to my side of the desk and knelt in front of me. He grabbed my hands and kissed them. I tried to hold back the tears, but at this point, I was emotionally spent. They started pouring out of my eyes once again. He touched my face and tried to smooth the tears away.

"If I could take back those words, I would, but it showed me I need to fix me. I don't know how to do it, but I can find a way if you tell me - promise me - I'll never see you leave like that again. Your face," he paused. Tears glistened in his eyes. I'd only seen that a handful of times since I'd known him. "When I saw you walk out the door, I wondered if you ever intended to come back."

"Drew, I've been in love with you since the first time you came to visit my brother. But I can't see you deal with your problems the way you're trying to. And if you're going to self-destruct, I can't stand back helplessly and watch you go up in flames."

He nodded.

"I've been trying to figure out what to say to you since you left. I don't know if I can fix everything right away. I don't know if I can make you any promises that everything will be the way it used to be."

He looked into my eyes. I believed that he wanted things to change.

"I wish I could work all of this out with you right now, but I have to go. I have a killer to find."

"Please. Drew."

"Please, promise me you will come home tonight."

"I promise."

He rose from his knees and pulled me out of his chair. He held me close to him.

"It may be late, but I'll be home tonight. I love you, Grace."

After he left, I glanced at the cupcake box on my desk, and I saw the Emmie's sketch of the butterfly next to it. I hoped he'd find the killer soon.

"I guess you won't be coming to my house tonight?" Emmie poked her head into my office.

"No, I won't be."

"They may be straws, but hold onto them, Grace."

I spent the rest of the day doing paperwork and praying for leads for Drew.

This evening would be the calm before the storm. Out of towners had already started arriving, and the exodus of Augustans had begun. Sunday was the one day of the week I was usually closed, but not this week, I had a dinner party to make arrangements for. So on this Saturday evening, we were taking it easy.

Drew wasn't as late as I thought he'd be. In fact, he wasn't late at all. He arrived at the same time I did. He'd stopped and picked up Chinese.

"Are you hungry? I have pepper steak, lo mein, and some sweet and sour chicken."

"It sounds wonderful. I think the only thing I've had today is a divine cupcake that someone brought to me."

"You have to stop and eat, you know."

"I suppose. I have so much to do. I got a fantastic opportunity this week with someone who is having several parties during the tournament. Her husband's company is in town for the week, and there are several events. She wants flowers and lots of them. I'll be able to give Emmie a bonus after this week."

"That sounds great, and it's good to see you smile."

He paused.

"Ken and Janice seem like nice people, and they seem really interested in helping those women."

It surprised me for him to bring the two of them up. I instantly liked them; however, there was something about the way Drew said that. It made me think he didn't quite trust them.

"Did they give you some good leads for around here?"

"Yes and no. I think they are keeping back some information because they want to help these girls, not get them arrested. It's hard to gain someone's trust if your information gets them thrown in jail. If Ken and Janice are telling the truth, they want those higher on the food chain to get arrested, not the girls they're trying to save."

"You don't think they are telling the truth?"

"Does anyone tell the complete truth?" he raised an eyebrow at me. "Their hearts may be in the right place, but they haven't come completely clean with me. They did give me a couple of leads, but almost all of the stuff they told me I already knew."

"Are they hiding something?"

He smiled.

"No one is ever as they seem in an investigation, Grace. You can't take anything or anyone at face value."

"That's kind of harsh, isn't it?"

"I'm sure they're good people, but you never know. They could be a front or a distraction. It could be the total opposite. They actually give up one or two of the working girls and let the big fish get away so the police are satisfied with making some arrests. I can't be sure."

"So what are you looking for?"

"I'm trying to solve a murder."

"You aren't interested in finding and helping these girls?"

"Of course I am, Grace, but my priority right now is to put a killer behind bars not expose a prostitution ring. If catching the killer means that happens, then that's a bonus."

The evening was quiet. It was if my explosion had never happened, and I wasn't sure that was a good thing. I couldn't let him sweep it under the rug. At least he didn't drink in front of me. I tried to sleep, but once again the dreams returned. This time I was back inside the beautiful home with all the girls inside. I could smell the heavy fragrance of magnolia. This dream didn't jolt me out of my sleep, but I did wake up. I turned to see Drew sleeping next to me, but it wasn't magnolias I smelled. It was the bourbon from the table in the living room.

8

Before this murder, I had what you might call a passing interest in Drew's job. I wanted to know about what he did, but I didn't want to help him solve a case. He shared too many gory details with me that I couldn't handle at the beginning of our relationship so he learned to tell me about cases but minus many details. I couldn't hear about domestic violence and child abuse cases. Those things were too hard. The less I knew the better - for me at least. This time it was different. Even though I didn't know Amber, I felt it was personal, and knowing that whoever did this to her was probably a visitor in my town throwing parties and selling these girls made it harder for me. I wasn't sure why. Maybe it was the dreams. They were so real, and I was caught up with what was taking place.

On Sunday afternoon, I headed into my shop. I let Emmie and Beth sit this one out because it was a small gathering, a supper club that had been meeting in individual homes for more than 40 years. Originally it had been 12 couples, but over time it had dwindled to eight, and during golf week, they had a special guest. They'd welcomed some big names in over the years. I was sure that there'd be no call girls at this event. It was quiet and dignified.

I made two large arrangements for their grand dining room table, and I was usually in and out of there quickly. But I'd known the hostess all of my life. She was a retired schoolteacher and had worked with my mother.

"So, who's the guest of honor this year?" I asked as I delivered the arrangements.

"It's a secret, my dear."

She put her forefinger in front of pursed lips. I smiled.

I think Mrs. Langham was in her late 70s, but she didn't look it. She was still in good shape, walking two miles every day. Her silver hair was perfectly coifed. She wore tailored pants and a simple three-quarter length cashmere sweater with a strand of pearls around her neck.

"How's your mother, dear?"

"She took an early retirement, and she's loving every minute of it. Baking, cooking and doing all sorts of stuff around her house. She's redecorated, and I think she's even writing a book."

I smiled, and Mrs. Langham laughed.

"She always talked about wanting to do all of those things," she said.

"And now she's getting the chance."

"I hear congratulations are in order for your husband," she said.

"Yes, he was promoted a couple of weeks ago."

"He's always been a fine young man. You know, I taught him in fourth grade."

"You were his favorite teacher."

She smiled.

"It's statements like that that made all of those years worth it," she smiled. "I always knew he'd do something to help people. He was always polite and courteous, and you could trust him to tell you the truth."

"That sounds like my husband."

She paused and glanced at the flowers on the table.

"They are lovely," she said.

I had the feeling she wanted to say something, but she seemed to be hesitating.

"Is something wrong, Mrs. Langham?"

"Yes, you could say that, I suppose."

"What is it?"

She looked around as though she was making sure no one was around to hear what she was about to tell me.

"We've always had the most gracious people rent the homes of our neighbors two doors down."

I nodded.

"I'm concerned this year," she said. "You see, last year, my daughter's neighbors made the mistake of renting out their home to someone who held some raucous parties. From what my daughter tells me, the guests were not only loud but..."

Mrs. Langham glanced around again and lowered her voice to a whisper.

"She said there were drugs and possibly prostitutes at the house."

She cleared her throat as the maid walked in the room. She'd brought the china in to place on the table.

"I'm sorry, Mrs. Langham," she said and scurried out of the room.

When she was out of earshot, Mrs. Langham continued.

"They caused a lot of damage to the home. I think my daughter called the police once. But the person who signed the agreement on that home and another has deep pockets so to speak. He paid for the damages and made a settlement with the home owner so they wouldn't talk about what had happened. But my daughter knew who was renting the house before all the hoopla occurred."

I nodded, hoping she'd get to the point.

"Now, through the grapevine I've heard that the same person who rented that home is now renting the house two doors down from us," she said.

"Okay."

"It's Bill Andrews, my dear," she said.

Bill Andrews. It seemed I couldn't get away from the Andrews family as hard as I tried. I never liked the man, but I put up with him for Dana's sake. I would not make a good detective. Tiny puzzle pieces got on my nerves.

"We don't want drugs and prostitution in our neighborhood this week. I know it happens, but not in my neighborhood. That happens in other parts of Augusta."

"So you want me to tell Drew for you?"

"Exactly. I know Drew has a lot of integrity. Plus, I know that he and Bill can't stand each other. Bill's deep pockets won't mean anything to your husband."

I laughed.

"You are so right on that one."

"Bill Andrews had such great parents. God rest their souls. And he has such a beautiful wife and new baby. I don't know what Dana Andrews sees in him."

I smiled.

"I'll pass the information on to Drew. Thanks."

I headed home and was surprised when I saw Drew there. I headed into the kitchen because I was starving, and I knew he had to be too. He followed me in and helped cut up some vegetables for a salad while I put some chicken in the oven to bake. I told him about Mrs. Langham and the address of her daughter which she'd written down for me.

"Do you think Bill Andrews could be mixed up in something illegal?"

"We've both known Bill all of our lives. If there's a big enough paycheck, I wouldn't put too much past Bill, but then again, he's never been arrested, and every allegation against him always disappears."

"Allegations? You've investigated him?"

"Not me in particular, but I know there have been questions."

Drew was deliberately vague.

"What kinds of questions?"

"Let's just say Bill has some high-powered attorneys who keep him one step ahead of the law."

"Mrs. Langham said he has deep pockets."

"Yes, he does."

"But murder? I mean, Bill isn't the nicest of people, but is he capable of killing someone?"

Drew put down his knife and looked at me.

"Greed does things to people. It's like a drug. The more money and power people get the more they crave. An addict will do anything for his next fix."

"Do you think this is related to the murder or does Mrs. Langham just want you to keep your eye out?"

"At this point, I can't leave any stones unturned. Did she give you the address?"

I nodded and gave it to him.

I wondered what Drew was hinting about. I really felt horrible about the way I'd treated Dana now. I knew Dana, and she never talked about anything amiss where Bill was concerned. But then again, he kept her in the dark about a lot of things. He made a lot of money. I could tell that from the home they lived in, the expensive cars they both drove and the jewelry he gave Dana. He had a computer software business I didn't know much about, and he also owned a medical equipment company. I did know he traveled extensively, but my relationship was with Dana not him. We typically didn't see each other if he was around, and then we managed to keep our conversation as far from our husbands as possible.

I tried to put Bill and Dana out of my head. I couldn't believe he was a criminal. Surely, Dana would know? But then again, he may have hidden it all from her.

9

Monday was uneventful as we got ready for the big day on Tuesday.

It was the first of Claire's parties. Emmie worked most of the day Monday on her gorgeous designs for it. Tuesday seemed to be working smoothly with the typical hospital runs, and Danny had been out delivering the orders for our other events. We had a couple of corporate parties.

"It's almost 2:30. We've got to leave," said Emmie.

"Let me try calling Danny again. We need the van."

I'd called his cell phone several times. Finally he answered.

"Grace, I'm sorry. I had a blow out. I couldn't answer because I was trying to fix it. I'm on Riverwatch Parkway now, and traffic is backing up. I can't tell what's going on up ahead. There must be an accident, and if there is, I'm stuck."

"It's okay. Emmie and I will take our own vehicles. If you make it back in time, can you mind the shop?"

"I can hang around until 4," said Beth. "But I'm really curious about this party you are going to. Is it the Italianate near the college?"

"I'm not sure which one it is. The address is in the computer on today's calendar," said Grace.

"I've been there before, but when Dr. Bailey owned it. When he retired and his wife died, he moved to retirement community in Evans. The person who owns it now is not from here, and there are rumors about his identity. He only comes in a few times a year. Mainly in March and April. I don't really know what he does. He's very secretive."

"I really don't know anything except that Claire is the one who made all the arrangements, and she's from Charleston. Would you like to come Thursday?"

"You bet I would. Sorry, Emmie, you can stay here."

Emmie laughed and shook her head.

"That is supposed to be the outdoor party," I said.

"If it's the one I'm thinking about, it's a gorgeous home, and the grounds are gorgeous as well. You wouldn't know it from the road, but it has a huge backyard so many of those historic houses on the Hill do. They are great places to have parties and convenient to the tournament as well."

"Well, as much as I'd like to chit-chat with you, Beth, Emmie and I have to go."

Traffic around town wasn't too bad during the off-peak times. It didn't take us nearly as long to arrive at the home as we'd thought it would. When we arrived, a housekeeper answered the door. We waited in the foyer. It was gorgeous with 16-foot tall ceilings, heart pine floors, and exquisite crown moldings. I loved the architectural details such as the medallions on the ceiling from which the ornate crystal chandeliers hung. The home was furnished with antiques. I wondered if the rugs really were antique Persian ones. From the foyer, I could see the grand staircase to the second floor and a study filled with bookcases. As I glanced around, I noticed a couple of young women standing at the top of the stairs. They were peering around the corner to see who was downstairs. When they realized they'd been spotted, they disappeared. I felt a chill on the warm April day.

"Wow," said Emmie. "I could get used to living someplace like this."

"You and me both. You could have one wing, and I'd take the other."

I felt like I should be whispering when I spoke because the

house seemed more like a library or museum than a place where someone might live.

It wasn't long before Claire met us in the foyer.

"So glad to see you," she said with a big smile.

"This is Emmie. Most of the work you saw was hers. She's amazing," I said.

"Pleased to meet you," said Claire, who once again was perfect from head to toe. She wore a floral-printed dress, and I was sure her nails and lipstick matched the dominant pink in the mix. In fact, I think the pink was the same color as a few of the flowers in the arrangements. I was almost surprised she wasn't wearing a wide-brimmed, Easter Sunday hat to match it. Maybe she would save that for the outdoor party.

"The arrangements are huge so we might need some assistance."

"Of course, I'll get someone," she motioned for the housekeeper.

Within a few minutes, two men wearing black pants and white long-sleeved shirts came out for the flowers.

"Be careful," instructed Claire as we followed her.

The dining room was expansive. One wall was filled with windows. I noticed several large magnolia trees outside the windows. A second chill went down my spine. I looked around the room. I'd never seen a dining room table that large. Two of the floral arrangements would go on the table, and the third was destined for the antique sideboard.

"This is absolutely gorgeous."

"Yes, hon, it's amazing. I wish I had a house like this. I might if my husband gets that promotion, and then, you'll have to travel to Charleston."

I liked Claire, but I was uneasy. I watched as the young men put the flowers on the table. I thought they were massive until they placed them on the table. The size of the table and the huge room dwarfed them.

Emmie checked to make sure none of the flowers were

damaged during the transporting of the arrangements and added a
few finishing touches.

"Grace, dear, I want to show you the site of Thursday's garden
party," said Claire.

I left Emmie as Claire led us outside through the sunroom to a
covered porch that spilled into the gardens. Beth was right. There was
no way anyone would have known how big this back yard was from
the street.

"We'll have several areas with food," Claire pointed to where
the different tables would be. "That's why I ordered the smaller
arrangements with the different flowers."

"Definitely, they will be perfect for out here."

"Thursday's party will be bigger, and I may have to go back to
Charleston for the day. I have some pressing business to attend to and
a meeting at 10. I should be back for the party itself, but all my plans
will have to be carried out before I leave or while I'm gone."

I followed Claire as she walked across the patio and down a
flagstone steps to the lower part of the yard.

"This probably won't be part of the soiree, but these grounds are
simply divine. I thought you might like to see them."

"Yes, thank you. It's beautiful."

"So be here by 2 on Thursday. The housekeeper will know
where everything is supposed to be, and you should have a good idea
as well."

As we walked back toward the house, I glanced up and saw
two women looking out of the upstairs windows. The curtains closed
quickly. I wondered if they were afraid of being seen. My imagination
started going in all sorts of directions. The house was strangely
familiar. Could it have been the one from my dream? I didn't have
many details of the house they were staying at in the dream - just
that it was a nice house with tall windows, magnolia trees, and scared
women. All of those fit except for the scared women part. I couldn't
tell about them as I looked up.

"We have several guests in the house with us," said Claire

almost as though she could read my mind. "They all work for my husband's company although there are some VIPs as well."

I nodded.

"We will have your designs here on Thursday, and you have a safe trip back to Charleston."

"Thank you, sweetie. I'll probably see you Sunday. That will be a huge soiree before everyone flies out on Monday."

"Thank you for your business."

"I'll be telling all my friends about you."

Emmie was waiting for me in the dining room. Once we got out of the house, I turned around to look at it. No one stared out of the windows. I tried to shake the feeling the women in my dream might be in that house, but other things didn't add up.

"Are you finished for the day?" Emmie asked.

"I haven't heard from Drew today. I don't expect him home anytime soon. I think I'll go back to the shop. I need to check on my orders."

"How is Drew?"

"I don't know. Nothing seems to have changed. He's still drinking. I woke up last night and could smell the alcohol. He got up after I went to sleep."

"Addictions aren't always easy to break."

"I know."

"My dad was a heavy drinker, and he tried so many times to quit. DTs can be bad. He's going to need you and some professional help to get through it. I keep telling you it's going to be fine. I know it will. Drew isn't stupid."

I nodded.

"Trust me. Trust him. Do you need me to come back to the shop with you?"

"Only if you want. Thank you for everything. Claire raved about your designs. I should have a really nice check for you by early next week."

"Listen, my kids are gone this week, and I have a couple of

MURDER UNDER THE MAGNOLIAS

commissions to do, but I'd really like to have another girls' night. Places are too crowded this week and the prices jacked up everywhere so you could come to my place."

"I'd like that. Drew's driven to solve this murder so I'm not sure when I'll see him again. Thanks, Emmie."

I headed back to the shop. Beth had locked up already, but I could open for another hour or so. I checked the cases for flowers. With what I had in the back and what I expected in on Wednesday, I should have enough for the orders. I was ready. I thought.

When I walked back to the front of the store, there was a young woman in the shop. I'd forgotten bells, and no one had come to fix the doorbell yet.

"Hi. I'm sorry I didn't hear you. Can I help you?" I asked.

She looked young. Maybe she was in her early 20s. I couldn't really tell. She had a pierced eyebrow and pierced lip. She wore her hair under a beanie. I could see that her bangs were black strands mixed with royal blue, and they covered her eyes. She had several tattoos including a small pink butterfly on her wrist. It wasn't nearly as ornate or as large as the dead girl's, but it was strikingly similar. I must've gasped when I saw it. She didn't seem surprised.

"I'm sorry. I don't mean to be rude. Your tattoo... I'm sorry I can't explain it."

"Yeah, I know. That's why I'm here," she said.

I didn't answer.

"I'm a friend of Amber's. Her name wasn't really Amber. It was Caroline Sims."

"C.S."

"Yes, but no."

"Why did you come here? How did you know?"

"I have ears, and I heard that a cop was looking for her. He came to Atlanta. I also heard about a woman here who was looking for a tattoo. People don't like to talk to cops, you know."

"Yes. I should call my husband."

"No. Look, I don't have much time. I convinced them to bring me down here. I have about 30 minutes to get back, but I had to find you."

"Convinced who?"

"Does it matter? The point is I'm here to give you some info."

I nodded.

"Does - did - Caroline have any family?"

"Her mom lives in New Orleans."

"How old was she?"

"She'd just turned 19. She came to Atlanta because some guy told her she could be a model. They just didn't tell her what type of a model."

The woman shook her head.

"It wasn't long before she was hooked on drugs, and then they wouldn't let her go home. She was theirs."

"What about you? Are you theirs too? What's your name?"

"Not important. You can call me Jay, like blue jay," she said pointing to the blue strand of hair.

"You don't have a name."

She shook her head.

"You're a nice lady and everything, but there are some things it's better that you don't know."

"You didn't answer me. Are you theirs too?"

"I've got to go."

"Why did you come here?"

"Bury her with a name, and tell her mom that she was a good kid."

"Can you tell me anything about the tattoo?"

"It was for her sister. She died from leukemia when she was 10. I can't remember her name, but those letters in the tattoo were her initials."

"Who would do this, Jay?"

Her mouth dropped at that question. I thought she might say something, but then she glanced over her shoulder. When she looked back, I could see the fear in her eyes. It was the same look I'd seen in the dead girl's face. Amber? Caroline? What was her name? Drew told me a few other possibilities. All these different names. I couldn't count how many there'd been for the dead girl, and now more names. Everyone told a different story. I couldn't keep up.

"I can't tell you. I've got to go now."

She turned to go, but I had to stop her.

"Wait. There are people who can help you."

"You mean those religious freaks?" she snickered as she said it.

I nodded.

"I don't believe their talk. Those success stories of theirs," she went on. "I mean, these girls they supposedly help - where do they go? They disappear off the streets, and you never see them again. They could be just as dead as Amber or worse. I've even heard that they take the girls and put them into their own setup, like a big commune or something in Montana. One man with lots of girls. That whole sister wives thing is just gross to me."

Jay shook her head.

"Sounds like some sick and twisted religious fanatics to me, and I've heard they get lots of money from somewhere," she continued. "Besides I'm not afraid of anyone. I'm a free agent. I do what I want, and I can quit when I want. And I have a gun that I'm not afraid to use."

"Do you really believe those people are the ones who killed your friend?"

"I never said she was my friend, and anything is possible."

"You wouldn't be here if she wasn't your friend, would you?"

"Like I said, Caroline was a good kid. She got mixed up with the wrong people. They said they were going to help her get off the streets. I guess they did. She's dead. She's not in the streets anymore."

She stared at me when she said that. I felt a chill.

"Please let me help you. Take my business card."

She stared at it for a minute and then handed it back.

"It wouldn't be safe for you, but I've got it here now," she said, pointing at her head.

"Can you tell me anything else about Amber - I mean, Caroline."

"Like I said, she was pretty, and they told her she'd be a model. She was really smart. She should've gone to school. She missed her mom. Her mom's name is Lucy."

"Let me help you. My husband - "

"Is a cop, and I don't want to go to jail."

"No. You wouldn't -"

"Cops put girls like me in jail. You seem like a nice lady so you don't have any idea of what cops are really like - on the job, that is. They're probably nice to you, but they aren't nice to people like me. Look, I've gotta go now."

She turned and walked out the door. I started to follow her when she turned and stopped me.

"Not a good idea to follow me. It could be bad news for you especially since you're a cop's wife."

I watched her walk down to the end of the street and take a right. Part of me was relieved, but another part of me was sad. I now had a name with a face. I hoped she was telling me the truth. When I walked back into the shop, I was surprised to see Emmie standing there.

"I didn't think you were coming back today."

"I left my phone here. I thought I'd left it in my car when we went to deliver flowers, but it was in the workroom. Are you going to call Drew?'

"You heard?"

She nodded.

"All of it."

I went over to the door again and looked out. I must've gasped or made a noise because Emmie was at my side all of a sudden.

"What's the matter, sweetie?"

"It's him," I said and pointed out the window.

"What's going on?" Emmie asked as I rushed into my office and pulled out my gun.

I headed for the door. I was going to confront this man until Emmie blocked the door.

"Have you lost your mind?" she asked.

I stared at her. I think I had lost my mind temporarily.

"If that man killed that girl, you need to let your husband handle this. He's the professional, remember?"

"He's outside now. He's the link to solving this murder. He'll get away, Emmie."

"I don't care. Drew can find him."

I tried to push my way past Emmie. She and I had both taken some self defense classes together, but she went further and got a few karate belts. She grabbed my wrist.

"I'm not letting you do something stupid. You're not a cop, Grace."

Emmie locked the door and closed the shop.

"Did you hear that girl who was here?"

"Yes, I heard it all."

"Maybe he was following her. Maybe she's in danger too."

Emmie pushed me into the workroom, and she locked the back door too.

"Call your husband," she said, shoving my cell phone into my hand.

I found myself getting mad at Emmie, but I wondered what I would've said or done if I'd come face to face with this man. Emmie disappeared as I tried to call Drew. He didn't answer. Now I was irritated with him.

"Drew, call me back. Emmie and I both saw the man this time. He's been by the shop. He's probably still out there."

"Everything is locked."

Emmie returned.

"I can't get Drew on the phone."

"Fine, we're just going to wait here in the workroom."

"But he's getting away."

"Let him. He killed someone - brutally killed someone. Have

you ever shot anyone, Grace?"

"I've only used this at the shooting range. I couldn't help Amber, but I could help Jay. Besides, I know he wasn't the one who pulled the trigger."

"I don't care. I'm not letting you put yourself in danger. How do you know that he didn't kill her?"

"My dream. I couldn't see the person, but it wasn't him. He knows who the killer is though."

Emmie stood with her mouth open. She shook her head at me.

"I don't know who this person in front of me is."

"Neither do I. Blame it on adrenaline," I said. I realized my hands were shaking as I tried to call Drew again. When he didn't answer, I resisted the urge to throw my expensive phone across the room.

"Jay said she wasn't afraid of them, but I think she was lying," said Emmie. "She sounded scared to me."

"That's what I thought too. I feel so helpless. I'm not a detective, but surely, there's something I could do to help these women."

"You help Drew find the murderer, and maybe that's something. Maybe he can pull down the people who did this and save the other girls they are forcing into prostitution."

"I hope you're right."

My cell phone began to ring - finally.

"What's wrong, Gracie?"

Gracie. He hadn't called me that in years.

"I think I might have an ID on our victim, and I think I saw the man we saw her with."

"An ID on our victim, Investigator Ward?" he asked with a laugh. "Don't move. I'm on the way."

"Emmie and I are locked in the storeroom with my gun. We aren't going anywhere."

"I'm glad to hear that. I'll be there soon."

Since Emmie was here, I had to ask her a couple of questions.

"Emmie, did you notice anything about the house we went to earlier?"

"Notice, as in how?"

"Did you see anything suspicious?"

Emmie shook her head slowly.

"Not really. Why?"

"I thought I saw some young women peeking at me from upstairs. Maybe I'm just getting paranoid now."

"I don't think you're paranoid, but now that I think about it, I did see a couple of women on the staircase when we first entered. They peeked around the top of the landing, but when they saw me looking, they ducked back."

My phone started vibrating.

"That was quick," said Emmie.

It was Drew, letting me know he was at the door, and he wasn't alone. He had brought reinforcements.

"You didn't have to bring the cavalry."

"You told me you saw a person of interest in a murder," he said.

"Yes."

"I saw him this time too, Drew," said Emmie.

"We're going to find him," he said before turning to me. "Now, I want you to tell me everything. And I'm going to need to get the security footage off your camera."

"Emmie was listening from the workroom so you may want to talk to her too."

It didn't take long to give Drew my statement. Emmie followed up with hers.

"We don't see anyone matching the description," a uniformed officer said as he walked into the shop.

"I'm taking you home, Gracie," Drew looked directly into my eyes.

"Are you done for the day?"

"Not really, but I'm taking you home. They know how to get me if they need me. You are more important to me right now."

106

"Don't worry about me. Go find this man. Surely he's somewhere close by."

Drew had the same look on his face that Emmie did only a few minutes before.

"I know, Drew. I don't know who this Grace is either. I think an alien came and replaced her," Emmie said.

He glanced at her.

"You just read my mind."

I hated that they were talking about me as though I wasn't even standing there. I was fine, and I didn't need to be coddled.

"I have a gun, Drew. Remember, you are the one who made sure I knew how to shoot it and that I had all the proper paperwork. Besides, how many cops did you bring down here to watch us? Go find the suspect."

"Butch, I'm taking my wife home," said Drew, completely ignoring everything else I'd said up to that point.

I let out an exasperated sigh.

"I'm not a little girl."

He walked over to me and touched my face.

"You will always be my baby."

"Fine."

We stopped for Chinese takeout and sat on the couch without saying much. I didn't understand how this person who called herself "Jay" had found me and why she came to me. All I could think of was Caroline or Amber, a young life snuffed out before its time. And then there was her mother. Two daughters lost. How horrible that must be, and she didn't know what had happened to her second daughter.

"Where are you, Gracie?"

"Gracie - you haven't called me that in years."

"I know. Somewhere along the way, I lost Gracie. Our relationship changed. I want Gracie back."

I leaned against his chest as he held me close. He was right. I was gone. In my mind, I'd traveled to New Orleans to meet Caroline's mother. I wondered about the girl who called herself Jay. Did her mother know what had happened to her little girl? How did Jay get mixed up in all of this? And then I wondered about my dreams. What if Ken and Janice were right, and there were other women in my city right now who were being forced into prostitution? What if Jay was right and Ken and Janice were tied to it?

"Drew, tell me what is going on with this investigation."

"I really shouldn't talk about it with you, babe," he said.

"Well we don't always do what we should, now do we?"

I sat up and looked at him. I didn't always ask prying questions about his work. I was happy not knowing about some of the things that happened in my hometown. Ignorance is bliss as they say.

"True, but you are in deeper in this than I like. The less you know the better."

"And you think I want to be here? I almost ran out of my shop today with my loaded gun to confront a murder suspect. I can't get the image of her dead body out of my mind. I can't let this happen to someone else. I keep dreaming about all of this. I've got to do something or else I'll go crazy. Now, I'm being watched. I've got someone visiting my shop out of the blue and knowing more about me than she should. Since I'm here, you need to tell me what else is going on."

"What do you mean?"

"Stop it, Drew. Just talk to me."

"We've already been through this. It's no secret golfers aren't the only ones making money this week. Legitimate businesses do very well, but some other illegitimate ones spring up as well. This tournament is a hot ticket. People know that the ones who come here pony up, and there's lots of money to be made. It gets bigger every year. I've gotten a few tips on some parties. Your friends, Ken and Janice, gave them to me. I've talked with them, and we could be making some arrests tonight. We've heard about a big party with lots of drugs and girls."

"Tell me something I don't already know. I know about these parties. I'm taking flowers to parties this week."

"I will check out any lead you give me."

"You don't need to be here with me now. These people will be gone when the tournament is over so you need to go."

Drew raised an eyebrow.

"Trying to get rid of me."

"No, it's not that, but you're on the clock. You know it. I know it. I'll be fine. I have my gun, and you've taught me how to use it. I shouldn't have called you. I was fine."

"Emmie told me that you were ready to chase down a murder suspect."

"Okay, I admit getting caught up in the moment."

"Is that what you're calling it?"

"Can I plead temporary insanity?"

"As long as you don't go through another incident of it any time soon."

I gave him a broad grin. We both knew it was fake.

"I promise to stay here."

He stared at me for a minute. I wondered what was going through his brain.

"They probably won't need me until a little later anyway so I'm going to stay here with you until I know you are okay."

"I'm okay. I can call Emmie if I sense another round of insanity coming on."

"I never thought I'd see the day when Emmie had the more level head of the two of you."

"Thanks a lot."

I laughed because I knew Emmie and I thought I knew myself.

Drew looked serious and perplexed at the same time with his head tilted and his eyebrows raised.

"It's taken a murder for me to see a different side of you."

"What?"

"I'm trying to figure out if I like it or not."

"You and me both, Drew."

10

Drew waited until I'd fallen asleep before leaving. I had a horrible dream. At least I think it was horrible. It was weird. I woke up with a start vaguely remembering the slamming of a door, and everything was dark. I wasn't sure if it was real or in my head. My heart was pounding, and I couldn't breathe. I wasn't sure why. As soon as I opened my eyes, I couldn't remember any of the details, but I knew I had to have dreamt of something. I turned to the clock. It was 12:53. I looked around the room. Drew wasn't in bed so I decided to go into the living room. It was empty. The slamming door was only in my dream. I walked over to our big comfortable couch and pulled out my journal. What would I write?

I sat there for a few minutes trying to force myself to remember. It wasn't long before it came flooding back to me. I knew why I'd immediately shut it out. In this dream, I wasn't sure where I was. Everything was dark around me. I stood up and tried to feel my way around a room. My neck and shoulders hurt. The doors were locked. I had a sense that now I was trapped just like the girls in my other dreams and then I heard the slamming of a door and train whistle. My heart started pounding.

It wasn't long before Drew walked in. He seemed surprised to see me sitting in the room.

"When I left you, you were sound asleep," he said as he walked toward me.

"Did your party turn up anything?"

"Not everything we were looking for, but there were some illegal drugs. Looked more like a frat party than anything."

I was seated next to his liquor cabinet. I noticed his hesitation. I could tell he wanted some of it. After wavering for a few minutes, he sat down next to me.

"Why are you awake?"

"I'm just going back to bed," I said as I started to stand up.

"What's wrong?"

I shook my head.

"Nothing. Insomnia, I guess."

I placed my dream journal on the table. I didn't have anything to write in it except the feeling that something bad was going to happen, and I headed back to our room. He followed me.

"Was it a bad dream?" he asked before I got to the bedroom door. I paused and turned to him, surprised he asked.

"I never mentioned anything about dreams, Drew."

"Come on, Grace. How long have we been married? I know you. I know what that book is."

He folded his arms against his chest and raised an eyebrow at me. I looked down.

"They all seem to be bad ones lately."

He took me in his arms, and I rested my head against him. I always felt safe when he held me close to him.

"I'm sorry. Do you want to talk about it?"

"There's nothing to tell really. I don't remember any of it."

He stepped back and raised my face to look into my eyes.

"Nothing?"

I nodded.

"Then how do you know it was bad."

"I think my heart is still racing. I woke up sweating, but then I had chills."

"Sounds like the flu, Gracie," he said trying to make a joke.

"I hope not."

"You need to know about a couple of parties I'm doing flowers for. I didn't think about this earlier," I said and told him in detail what I'd seen at Claire's party. "I have another one Thursday or I guess that's tomorrow, but I don't know if there's anything to this house or not. She seems like the epitome of the proper Southern lady. I can't imagine her being involved in something like that. Most of the other parties I'm doing are stodgy, corporate things. But you told me not to take anything or anyone at face value."

"Claire might not know what all is going on."

"I've thought that. I don't want you raiding this party without any hard evidence. Great, I'm more worried about losing a customer than what's really important," I sighed.

"It's okay, babe. I don't think you meant it that way."

I shook my head.

"It's almost like the parties are one place, and the girls are being kept another place. At least they are in my dreams. They might show up at the parties before they start, but they don't stay in the houses where the parties are held. I've had several dreams and heard train whistles."

Drew laughed.

"Babe, this is Augusta. There aren't too many places around where you don't hear trains."

"You don't hear them on the Hill really. That's the one place in town that seems to be train-free."

"True. You've given me a lot of stuff to go on today."

"Thanks for listening to me."

"Your dreams aren't concrete evidence though. You know I can't use them."

I smiled.

"Maybe not. But you and I both know they're real."

He narrowed his eyes at me. I could tell this conversation wouldn't end well if I said anything else, and I didn't feel like fighting with him at 1 o'clock in the morning. There was a time and place to cross that bridge, and it wasn't now.

"Why don't we talk about this another time?" I asked as I headed to bed.

Drew was gone a few hours later. He wanted to beat the traffic that gnarled Washington Road and Riverwatch Parkway heading into downtown Augusta. I took alternate back roads into the shop.

With the practice rounds on Monday and Tuesday, it was time for the Par 3 on Wednesday morning. The Par 3 Tournament was a tradition dating back to 1960, and in its history, no golfer had ever gone on to win both the Par 3 and the overall tournament in the same year although some tournament winners had won the Par 3 in other years. Sometimes golfers even let their children play caddie for them. But golf wasn't on my platter Wednesday even though it was for most of the rest of the city. I had a few things to take care of for Thursday's party but not enough to bring in Beth. She only wanted to go to the different parties during the week to check out the interior of other people's houses. Emmie would be in in the morning. There were some get-well arrangements as well as new baby ones. There was also another one congratulating Dana Andrews. Danny would be busy delivering flowers. I still wasn't up to seeing Dana quite yet even though I really wanted to be happy for her.

"Dana Andrews is popular. Do you know how many of these arrangements I've made and haven't told you about?" Emmie asked as she looked over my shoulder at my computer screen.

"So does that mean you are up for another?"

"I can, but at some point, you're going to have to go over there to see her."

"Yes, Mom, I will."

I turned to her when I said that. Her face turned red as she glanced at me.

"I'm sorry, Grace."

"Don't worry about it."

"No really. I am. I shouldn't have said that. "

"Emmie, I really am happy for her, but part of me just can't handle it right now."

She gave me a quick hug.

"I'm sorry. I'm your best friend, and while I like not having to share you with Dana anymore, I know that she misses you too. She's asked me what's wrong. It really bothers her that you won't talk to her. She thinks she's done something wrong, and it's not my place to tell her."

"Thanks, Emmie. It's okay. I just feel like such a horrible person for being so jealous of her."

"I'm sorry, sweetie."

"I know. My brother's wife is having another baby too. It seems like everyone is except me. I'm sorry to be so depressing. Let's talk about something else."

Emmie gave me a weak smile and changed the subject.

"Any leads on our killer?"

"None that Drew is telling me about."

"You can't use your charms to get information out of him?"

I laughed.

"He said he's trying to protect me by not telling me anything. I guess I understand that. Besides he told me I gave him enough leads to keep him busy. He didn't go to bed until after 1, and I think he was out the door around 4."

Emmie looked up. I noticed as the blood seemed to drain from her face.

"What's wrong?"

"Speak of the devil."

"What are you talking about?"

As I turned, I realized why she looked as she did. It was Bill Andrews - Dana's husband, and he didn't look happy. He was wearing clothes that were more appropriate at the tournament - plaid pants and a hot pink golf shirt. No one dressed like that unless golf was on the menu. I'm sure he was heading that way, but why was he here now?

Emmie walked out to the front.

"Where's Grace?" he asked brusquely without even

acknowledging Emmie. He was the absolute last person I expected to see in my shop because I knew he was busy with out-of-town guests this week and for other personal reasons.

"Hi, Bill," I walked out of my office.

He narrowed his eyes and glared at me. He was not happy to see me.

"I'm only here because Dana insisted I come here to see you," he said.

"What can I help you with?"

"Do you know how upset Dana is that you haven't even acknowledged our daughter's birth?"

I didn't say anything. What was there to say? I bit my tongue and braced myself for the verbal lashing I was getting ready to receive.

"Don't you have anything to say for yourself?"

All I could do was tell myself not to cry right now. I repeated it in my brain several times. I would not allow Bill to bully me into crying. He wouldn't get the satisfaction.

"Bill, is there something we can help you with?" Emmie stepped in.

"She wants to bridge the gap with you, Grace, and she thinks that she did something wrong so she sent me here to appease you."

He paused. I couldn't respond because I didn't think I could say anything without breaking into tears.

"I got a client last minute, and Dana seems to think we need flowers at this. I think we have enough flowers. Our house has become an extension of your floral business lately, but that's another story. Dana also seems to think you are the best in town despite the fact that there are dozens of other florists. I really don't think flowers are going to impress anyone, but because I love my wife, I'm here. Believe me there's nothing I'd rather do than tell people never to come here."

"Thanks for the vote of confidence," Emmie said.

"No one is talking to you, Emmie," he blasted at her.

He looked back at me.

"Did you even know Dana almost died in the middle of her C-section?"

I looked down. I didn't know that.

He wrote something down on a piece of paper.

"Here's the address for the party tomorrow. Obviously, it's not at my house. The party starts at 6 so I need you there and gone before the guests arrive. I don't need the help there mixing with the important people. Ask for my assistant, Olivia. Here's my card. I want the best you've got."

I couldn't move as Emmie took care of the details.

"I'm glad to see this conversation has bothered you. It should. Dana has always considered you one of her best friends, and you abandoned her when she needed you most."

With that comment, Bill left the building, and the stupid tears came back again. Emmie hugged me.

"Don't let him hurt you. You and I know the truth."

"He's right. I am a horrible person," I could barely choke the words out.

Emmie let me go and stared right into my eyes.

"You're not a horrible person, but he doesn't understand what you are going through because you never bothered to talk to Dana."

I nodded.

"I just didn't know what to say to her. I didn't want her feeling sorry for me."

"I will take care of these flowers."

"Let me see that address."

I stared at it. It was down the street from Claire's, and it was not the address Mrs. Langham had given me. She did mention that he'd rented a couple of houses last year.

"The Hill is a popular spot this week."

"Apparently. Listen, I can deliver it so you don't run into him again. I never understood what Dana saw in that jerk to begin with."

"It certainly wasn't his charming personality."

"You can say that again."

"Are you talking about Bill Andrews?" Beth had come in through the back of the shop without either of us knowing.

"How did you guess?"

"I saw him leaving in his brand new sports car. I don't see how they will fit a car seat in that one."

"Yes, he paid us a pleasant social visit," said Emmie sarcastically.

"Are you okay, Grace?" Beth asked.

"Peachy."

"I should've said something sooner."

"What are you talking about?"

"He's getting you to do flowers for his party?"

I nodded.

"I don't know why this didn't click earlier," she almost sounded as though she was talking to herself and not to us.

"What, Beth?"

"Something he said to my husband just came back to me."

"What are you talking about?"

"Bill likes the ladies a lot, and I've heard that some of his clients have the same tastes."

"Well, I think we've all known he was a womanizing creep. He tried to hit on me when he and Dana first started dating. When I wouldn't fall for whatever charm he thinks he possesses, he turned a cold shoulder to me. He's hated me ever since," I said.

"It's more than that. His tastes have gotten more expensive and specific, and he likes to talk about some of his conquests in the golf locker room. You know he and my husband used to play golf together. My husband stopped playing with him because one night Bill got too drunk after winning and told him how he paid for some high-dollar call girls while in Japan."

"You think he might have some entertainment, so to speak ,for his clients?"

"That's exactly what I think," Beth put her hands on her hips.

I knew Bill was a jerk, but a criminal mastermind? I really didn't think he was smart enough. Bill was climbing quickly to the top of my most hated list. If all this was true, he was slime. I was still torn about seeing Dana, but now, could I hold back info on her husband from her? I was about to get on the phone with Drew when Ken walked in.

"Where's your other half?" I asked, wondering where Janice was.

"We rescued a girl last night, and Janice is with her now."

"That's awesome. I wish there was more that I could do."

"Who knows? Maybe you will."

The words struck me as strange. It's like it ignited some dormant thoughts in me that I didn't know existed. They were almost prophetic. I'd always wanted to do something meaningful and important with my life. Maybe I'd met Ken and Janice for a reason.

"Why do you say that?"

"Well, another part of the reason we're here is to start up an effort here. This goes on even when the golfers leave."

I nodded.

"So maybe you can be part of that?" he asked.

"I think I'd like that, and I'll do whatever I need to."

For some reason those words hit me. It wasn't a cliché. I felt I might have to own up to them.

11

Thursday - the first day of the tournament and Claire's big garden party that evening and Bill's event.

Drew wanted me to keep my eyes open at both parties to see if I noticed anything unusual. Part of me had wished I hadn't said anything about Claire's party. I couldn't say the same thing about Bill. I imagined being wrong and several uniformed deputies crashing Claire's event to find nothing. And losing potential business when Claire found out. I could worry sometimes. I came from a long line of professional worriers.

Beth was excited about Claire's party. She had her own events she was attending that night, but she begged to help me deliver the flowers to it. She'd chatted non-stop about it as we finished the flower arrangements on Thursday morning.

"I am dying to see the inside of this house and the gardens. They went downhill the older Dr. Bailey got. He couldn't keep up with them, and he had someone only do the bare minimum of trimming hedges and cutting grass. The new owner has had several months to get them in shape, and my neighbors have told me that they've seen several trucks from area nurseries going behind the gates."

"Beth, they really are lovely gardens."

"Some of the camellias in my yard came from his. Those camellias have history with them."

I nodded.

"And what about the inside. Mrs. Bailey, God bless her, had

gaudy taste. The wallpapers were atrocious, but that does go in line with the Victorian theme she had. They liked things like that. But to use a Victorian - Queen Anne theme in an Italianate style house... It just didn't work. She was over the top in her decor, but my grandmother and Mrs. Bailey were best friends. That's how I know so much about the house. I went there a lot as a child."

"I can say this - the theme of the decor does a better job of matching the architecture now," said Emmie.

Beth put down her flowers and picked up her phone.

"I need to delete some photos," she said.

"Beth, you can't take any photos in this house. We're working," I said.

"I'd love to put them on my blog."

"No, you can't do that either."

She smiled at me and gave me a wink.

"Fine. I have other ways, you know."

"Good. Use your other ways. Don't get me into trouble."

"You need to loosen up a little. We're going to a party."

"We aren't going to the party itself just to the house where the party will be."

"You really are no fun, Grace."

"Let's just get these flowers finished."

I wasn't sure what I was supposed to be looking out for at this party. When we arrived, the housekeeper let us in, and Beth and I took the flowers to the locations where Claire had pointed out. I noticed Beth making mental notes of all of the decor. She had a photographic memory when it came to anything related to home decor. She wrinkled her nose a couple of times at a few pieces. I could tell she was thinking about what she'd do differently. I'd have an earful on the drive back to the shop.

I needed to stall somehow so I could be in the house long enough to pick up anything that might be a lead for Drew. We did need to replace a few flowers that had gotten damaged during the drive.

As we were placing the flowers, Claire and her effervescent presence arrived. She headed straight for one of the large centerpieces and leaned in with her eyes closed to take in the aroma of the roses and other blooms.

"Oh, I'm so glad I made it back in time to see you bring everything in," she exclaimed. "These are simply divine."

She hugged me.

"Better than I could've imagined," she said.

Claire wasn't alone. Two young women walked in with her. They could have been models or beauty queens. I could envision them with tiaras on their heads and beauty pageant sashes. Both of them were tall and slender with perfect tans. One had platinum blonde hair and the other had long, rich chestnut brown locks. They were both wearing dresses and heels so high that I knew I couldn't put on without tripping and breaking an ankle.

"Do you ever think about coming to Charleston? I'd love to have your designs there. So different. And I never would think to use those flower and color combinations, but they work so well together."

I smiled. I'd have to tell Emmie. She'd be thrilled to hear such praise. I should've brought her along, but Beth had insisted.

"Thanks."

I tried not to stare at the two women who came in with her. They talked to each other as though Beth, Claire, and I weren't even in the room. The blonde covered her mouth as she leaned closer to the brunette. The two giggled and then looked at us as if sharing in some kind of private joke. With no warning, they turned and left the room.

Claire was oblivious to them as she continued to rave about the flowers.

"You know, you and I should have lunch together sometime in Charleston. I know the best places. We could expand your business some."

I nodded as Claire's phone began to ring.

"Excuse me," she said as she turned.

I tried not to be rude, but I couldn't help hearing her side of the conversation.

"What do you mean they can't be delivered? Well that just won't do at all," her sweet, melodic voice dropped into an angry growl.

I looked at Beth who slightly shrugged her shoulders.

"We have to have them here," Claire continued and began to walk away. "The men coming tonight have been promised certain things, you know. We want them to have a good time. We can't disappoint them."

The hair on the back of my neck stood on end and a knot formed in the pit of my stomach as she said that. I tried to distract myself with picking up stray pieces of greenery that had fallen off onto the table.

She continued to talk, but she'd moved out of range. I glanced at Beth again. She shook her head. She didn't hear anything either.

"Pardon me," Claire said as she got off the phone. Her voice was back to the one I had heard before, and her plastic smile had returned. "The big party is Saturday night, and those designs I picked out have to be perfect. I did tell you I added another party on Saturday, right? Not just the final one on Sunday. After seeing these, I know they will be. We are supposed to have some golfers and their wives for this. Also, we have some very important foreign dignitaries coming."

No, she hadn't said anything about another party. Foreign dignitaries? What were the men promised for tonight? And she specifically said men.

"We'll be here. Emmie has a few things in mind that I know you'll love."

"Emmie's the star of this operation?" Claire tilted her head as she asked the question with a smile.

"Grace is a true Southern lady - modest and willing to give her spotlight away to her friends," Beth chimed in.

"Oh stop it, Beth."

"It's true. Emmie is talented, but Grace is the creative brains

122

behind everything. That's why we love her so."

Beth smiled.

The arrangements were in place and looked amazing. I wanted to linger, but I couldn't think of anything else to say. The phone conversation wasn't enough for the police to crash the party over especially when I only heard one side of it.

"What time Saturday?"

"3 is good again."

"See you then."

"I'll walk you outside," Claire offered.

"You don't have to -" I started to say.

I wondered if she offered to see us out so we didn't have a chance to look around anymore, not that we'd seen anything. This seemed to be a dead end, and we had little time.

"Nonsense, " she replied and handed me a piece of paper. "Here are a couple more items I need for Saturday, and my card number is on there too."

I nodded and tried to keep my eyes straight ahead. I wondered if Beth had seen anything.

I didn't say anything until I'd started the van and gotten out of the driveway.

"So what do you think?"

"I'd love to know what they promised those men coming to the party," she said dryly.

"I know. I supposed it could have been anything - beer, for example, or chicken wings."

"No alcohol would be a party ender for Claire. It could even be drugs."

"Did you see anything else? Those women who came in with Claire didn't seem to be there against their wills."

"No, they seemed happy to be there."

Our next stop was the location of Bill's party. We had two large arrangements to bring in, plus some smaller ones. He'd changed his order three times before the event. I had wanted to call Dana now more than ever, but I wasn't going to do it because of her bullying husband.

Bill's event would be held on the grounds underneath large air-conditioned white tents. I noticed the beautiful magnolia trees in the back. They had to be a couple hundred years old. They were huge, but magnolias were common in this part of town. I think every yard we passed had at least one.

Olivia was nice enough. I guess she had to be considering her boss.

"We've got the tables up. I'll have someone help bring the arrangements in."

Beth and I had brought some of the smaller ones in and placed them on the tables where she directed us. We exchanged pleasantries, but there wasn't time for much talk. I tried to discreetly look around. Bill was a sneaky type. There wouldn't be much evidence just lying around.

As we headed back to the house, I looked up. I didn't see anything out of the ordinary, no figures at the window peeking through curtains, nothing.

Drew wasted no time before calling to check on our outing. I told him about the conversation we'd overheard at Claire's and the women we saw at Claire's, but he said what I thought he would that there was nothing concrete to go on.

"I have another lead from Janice and Ken tonight. I'll call you if anything turns up," he said.

"Okay."

We headed back to the shop to return the van to its parking spot. I wished there was something I could do to solve this or help Drew. Emmie was still at the shop. She'd keep me company for the next hour or so.

"Well, Grace, I've got a party to go to, but I'll keep my ears and eyes open for you," said Beth. "Got any plans for tonight?"

"No. Maybe Emmie and I will watch a movie and have ice cream."

"I'll see you for a couple of hours in the morning."

"How did it go?" Emmie asked.

"Nothing exciting."

"Do you think there's something going on in either of those houses?"

"I don't know. Claire got a phone call and I heard her say the men were promised certain things. They could've been promised crab legs for all I know. It could be anything."

Emmie laughed.

"You're probably right," she said. "But you have a look on your face."

"What look?"

"Don't try to play innocent."

I did have a thought - a crazy one. I smiled.

"Maybe we could drive by there?"

Emmie smiled. She tilted her head to the side and stared at me.

"Who are you, and what have you done with my best friend?"

"What are you talking about?" I laughed as I asked the question.

"I don't know who this Grace is. I mean, in high school, there was a glimmer of a Grace who craved adventure, a Grace I almost pulled out of her shell, but you were always too shy to do anything about it. But now - the other day you wanted to chase a killer, and now you're up to something, but I don't know what that is," Emmie said with her head tilted to the side as though she was trying to sum me up.

After a few second, Emmie winked at me.

"I'm so glad to know I've finally rubbed off on you. It certainly did take long enough."

She started to laugh.

"Even Drew said something about that the other night. He said it was bad when you were the more level headed of the two of us."

"Thanks a lot, Drew. I love you, too, wherever you are," she said sarcastically.

"Emmie, there are women who are in trouble," I tried to be serious. "If I don't help them, I will regret this all of my life. Drew is running out of time. Whoever is behind this will be gone in a couple of days. It'll be over. Unless it's Bill Andrews, but the people he's working with will be gone."

Emmie shook her head.

"Tell yourself it's for the good of someone else all you want, but you know you want to have an adventure. I can see it in your eyes."

She paused for a moment as though she was trying to think of something.

"I wish there was some way to crash these parties, but people at both parties know both of us," she said.

"Since when were you ever cautious?" I giggled. "Maybe I've rubbed off on you."

Emmie had given her adventurous side too much leeway in the past, but she'd mellowed some with age.

"You got me there. I haven't crashed a party in a long time. Maybe I'm the one in need of adventure."

"Well, we aren't exactly going to crash a party - just spy on Claire's. I can't risk going near Bill's party - not after seeing him yesterday. "

Emmie nodded.

"He's a horrible man. You shouldn't have agreed to do these flowers for him."

"Maybe not, but if he's got a taste for expensive call girls, he could be mixed up in this."

"So what's the plan then?"

"Well, I did notice a thing or two while we were there at the house. One is that the next door neighbor is an elderly man with no animals in his back yard. He has a cat. I saw him outside with the cat, but there are no dogs. There's a lot of hedges in the back and a fence that doesn't look too difficult to jump over. If we wear black and go after dark, maybe no one will notice."

Emmie laughed.

"We could splash a little alcohol on us, and if anyone confronts us, we could pretend to be drunk."

"Grace, you're starting to think like me," she grinned. "You know you're crazy, right?"

"Is that a bad thing?"

"No, I think your heart is in the right place, but there is one thing that concerns me."

"That is?"

"What about Drew?"

"What about him? I'm doing this to help him."

"Are you sure?"

"What do you mean? You and I can't arrest anyone. If I saw anything, I'd have to let him know."

"You know he wouldn't approve."

"I know that, but maybe we could call in an anonymous tip."

Emmie raised her eyebrow at that one.

"Come on, Emmie, Drew is not the only deputy in the Augusta-Richmond County sheriff's department that I know. And if I saw something, I could call someone else."

"He'd still know."

I sighed.

"Now, who's the one who isn't any fun?"

Emmie laughed.

"We've switched places - the irony of it all."

Emmie put her hands on her hips.

"I know, but like I said I can't sit back and do nothing. If these people are just bringing the women in for the tournament, we don't have much time. Besides, Drew doesn't have to know unless we find something."

"And then what are you going to tell him?"

"I'll figure that out if it comes to it. We have to find something first, and if we do, then I'll worry about trespassing charges."

"Okay, Miss Detective, I'm game."

"Great. I'll see you around 7. We've got a party to crash."

MURDER UNDER THE MAGNOLIAS

12

I picked Emmie up around sunset. I kept thinking I'd seen too many spy movies, and I probably had. The idea of those women from my dream and the reality of Amber or Caroline or whatever her name was drove me to do this. I couldn't help myself.

There were lots of cars on the side streets near the mansion. The front of the home seemed quiet. The trees surrounding the deep lot muffled the sounds from the back yard although there was a fairy-like quality with the twinkling lights coming from the back yard. I'm sure Claire was an expert hostess, and she didn't need to see us. We walked toward the house as though we intended to go to the party; however, we slipped through the neighbor's gate instead, heading toward a row of boxwoods and azaleas. As we approached, the sounds of a jazz band grew louder.

"Where are we going?" Emmie asked.

"We're going to hide somewhere in the bushes."

I brought a pair of binoculars with me. I wasn't sure if they'd be any use.

"Sweetie, what are we looking for?"

I shook my head.

"I'm not really sure, but I think we'll know if we see it."

It wasn't a wild party by any means. There were women there, but they definitely didn't look like prostitutes. The two women from earlier were beauty queens, tiaras, sashes and all. I couldn't tell what titles they'd won. Most of the women were clumped together in small groups, chatting amongst themselves, sipping on wine, and paying no attention to the men attending.

The men also were in small groups. Many of them were drinking beer and eating chicken wings. The binoculars were a huge help, and the food looked really good. The people at this gathering were comfortable with each other as though they were close friends. In fact, I recognized several of my customers in the mix. There were still some Augustans who stayed in town for the tournament and used their badges instead of selling them or allowing others to use them.

"Well, this is definitely not the right party," I said to Emmie after a few minutes.

"Are you sure?"

"Yes, you and I know some of the people in the crowd. Actually, I think we know most of them. Maybe this really is a business gathering. It's really staid."

"Okay. I'm ready to leave then. It really should be too early for mosquitoes, but something is biting me. Being a spy isn't as fun as I thought it would be."

"Ants?"

"What do you mean, ants?"

"Biting you."

"I hope not."

"I wonder what Claire was talking about when she said they couldn't disappoint the guests."

"I have no idea. It had to have been beer," said Emmie. "I have ivy in places where it shouldn't be, Grace."

Just then, Claire appeared.

"Who is that with her?" Emmie asked.

"I can't tell. Judging by those clothes though, I'd say it was a golfer. He's kinda cute."

"Let me see," Emmie grabbed the binoculars. "Oh yeah, he's a hottie all right. I think I saw his picture in the paper today. He definitely looks like a golfer, and there's another one with him."

I could hear what sounded like clapping.

"Emmie, you're strangling me with the binocular strap."

"Oh sorry. Well I was hoping for something James Bond like tonight, and we ended up with Lucy and Ethel."

"Isn't that the truth?"

"So I guess the golfers were the special guests they needed to deliver tonight?" Emmie asked.

"I guess."

"Let's go, Grace. This has been a waste of time."

"What about Bill's party? Do you think we could get there?"

"I feel icky. I'm sweaty and dirty. Spying is so much more glamorous in the movies."

I picked a leaf out of Emmie's long brown hair.

"Ugh, you mean I'm going to have to wash my hair?"

She sounded disgusted.

"Remind me never to go on a camping trip with you."

"Camping, please. Have you ever seen me camping?"

"No, you're right."

I paused.

"Let's at least drive slowly past the house where Bill's party is."

I think I sounded like I was begging.

"I don't think we'll be able to see anything, and I certainly don't want to get any closer to anyplace where Bill Andrews is. I've never liked that man, and after the way he treated you when he came in the other day, I don't want to risk another run in. I hope Drew gets something out of that information you gave him," Emmie said.

We made a b-line for my car, but as we got closer, my heart started to race. Someone was standing next to my vehicle. It was dark outside. And the towering trees lining the street cut out the moonlight. I couldn't tell who is it was. There was no street lamp near where I parked. I moved closer to Emmie and grabbed her hand. She glanced at me, and I nodded in the direction of the stranger at my car. I reached into my pocket to make sure my phone was there. I couldn't tell in the dark if it was the man from the parking lot or not.

That seemed so long ago.

I was just going to walk past the car without stopping, but as I got closer, I could see the person's profile. It was Drew, and he had his arms folded across his chest. That was never a good sign. He only did that when he was angry.

"Grace."

His voice was low - that was another bad sign.

"Hi Drew, nice night for a walk," said Emmie.

"Take Emmie home, and I'll meet you at our house," his voice sounded deeper than usual and calm. I knew I was in trouble. If we ever did have kids, that would be the "you're grounded until you're 18" tone.

He stood in front of my door for a minute. I couldn't look at him. I felt like I was about 10 years old. He didn't say anything, and then he stepped aside from the driver's side door so that I could get in. He didn't move completely out of the way until I'd turned on the vehicle.

"Why do I feel like I'm 16 and just got caught coming in through my bedroom window after meeting Jake Skinner at the late movies?" Emmie asked.

"You really did that? I thought that was just a rumor."

"No, that was the truth, but it was the only time I was caught," she grinned at me. "You were probably home reading or something."

"Can I blame you for this then?"

Emmie laughed.

"Sorry, honey, you are on your own with this one. I can't even be in the room with you to make a case for you."

"I know. Say a little prayer for me, will you?"

I pulled up to Emmie's house. She didn't live too far from the party.

"I will. It's going to be okay. I'm sure once he realizes how much you care about finding these traffickers he'll soften."

She leaned over and gave me a quick hug.

"Thanks."

132

"Call me and let me know what happened."

It didn't take long to get home, but I drove well below the speed limit to avoid this as much as possible.

Drew hadn't turned on the lights when I walked in. I could see him as the moonlight cut through the blinds. He was sitting in the shadows waiting for me.

"So should I call you Nancy Drew now or is this another case of temporary insanity?"

His sarcasm cut through the darkness.

"No," I whispered. I felt like a teenager again. I knew it wasn't a good idea to spy on the party."Look, Drew, I'm sorry. I feel stupid now, but what if I'd found something? You're only one person, and the sheriff's department can't be everywhere all at one time."

He didn't answer. Instead, he stood up and walked toward me. He put one hand on each of my arms.

"Grace, you let me do my job. I can't do that if you are going to keep doing stuff like this. Please don't put yourself in danger," his voice wasn't angry at all. Instead, I heard a soft anguished cry pleading with me. "You don't know what you're up against, and neither do I."

"I can't help it. I don't want to see another life destroyed. I don't want to see another woman dead."

"What were you going to do?"

"I don't know. I just wanted to see if there was anything I missed. I was going to call you or leave an anonymous tip with Butch if I saw anything out of the ordinary. Our flowers looked like they were the best part of that party."

Drew laughed.

"We had someone undercover there. He said the same thing."

Drew pulled me close to him and stroked my hair.

"Grace, I love you, but these are dangerous people. You don't seem to understand this."

I pulled back. I wondered why he felt the need to remind of this. He must've known something he wasn't telling me. He was a little too overprotective.

"What about Bill's party?"

"I don't know anything yet. If Beth and Mrs. Langham were right about the call girl thing, then there could be something to this party. Obviously, I couldn't go to it because I know Bill. I just thought I knew him better than that."

"I don't have any reason not to believe Beth."

"No, Beth is a credible source of gossip."

"Did you find anything else?"

"It's possible, but it's in Columbia County not Richmond. And it only concerns me if they find something associated with our homicide investigation. We've got open lines of communication with them."

"Gated communities."

"What?"

"It was something that Ken said. Something about gated communities and so did Mrs. Langham. Bill's party was in a gated community last year."

"Well, there is someone looking in that direction tonight. We're going to find this killer and this ring."

"There's not much time, Drew."

"I know that, sweetheart."

His phone began to ring. He looked at the number.

"This could be the call I've been waiting on."

He turned away.

"Yeah, Ward here," he said.

I tried to listen to the conversation, but Drew didn't say much just a few "yeses" ending with an "I'll be there soon." When he finished the call, he turned back to me.

"It's a lead, a weak lead, but a lead," he said.

He pulled me close to him.

"I'm not sure when I'll be back, but don't do anything foolish while I'm gone. I've been doing this a lot longer than you."

I nodded.

He touched my face and tilted my chin up so I could look at

him.

"Gracie, I'm not angry. I just don't want anything happening to you. This isn't like you. You aren't usually the adventurous type."

"I know."

He gave me a kiss.

"Don't wait up."

I followed him to the door and watched him leave. I picked up my phone to text Emmie and let her know that I hadn't been arrested or anything. I decided to take a shower after climbing into the azalea beds at the house on Walton Way, and once I got out, I noticed a strange text on my phone.

It said it was from Jay and that she had some info.

It wasn't even 9. It seemed like it should be much later than that.

I wondered what I should do after Drew's plea for me to stay put and safe.

She wanted me to meet her at a diner downtown. It was a public place. Surely I would be safe. I'd been to that diner before. There were security cameras inside and often a deputy or two. I put my gun in my purse just in case. Before I left, I tried calling Drew, but I didn't get any response.

When I arrived at the diner, I didn't see too many cars. Fortunately, I was able to park close and slip inside in no time. I saw Jay sitting at one of the booths. She was looking down at a cup of coffee.

"What's wrong?" I asked as I sat down.

She looked up at me. One of her eyes was black and her lip cut and swollen.

"Do you need me to take you to the hospital?" I asked.

"No," she said and shook her head.

She slid a locket across the table and a piece of paper.

"This belonged to Amber," she said.

"Shouldn't you be giving it to the police?" I asked.

It was a heart-shaped pendant. I remembered seeing it on her the night in the parking lot. I wanted to open it, but it was evidence. I didn't need to tamper with it.

"I've already told you. Cops don't like people like me. Besides, you're married to a cop so you're the next best thing."

"What's this paper?"

"I heard about this party tomorrow night. I was asked to go to it, but my boss and the guy running the party - let's just say they don't see eye to eye. And look at me now, I can't make any money with this face. They want something a little more upper crust. I can't fake that with my piercings and hair. Now this. Makeup does a lot, but not for a couple of days."

I opened the paper to see the address. It was a house down by the river. Maybe that explained the trains I heard in my dream?

"Jay, where are you from? Do you have any family?"

"My family is from the street, and I'm going back to them. I made a few bucks earlier this week."

"Who did this to you?"

"Not my boss, but the other guy. When he found out who I worked for, he sent me with a message."

"Let me buy you some coffee."

"Thanks."

She looked at me for a moment.

"People don't do nice things for people like me unless they want something."

"Then you've been hanging around the wrong people."

She gave me a weak smile.

"I live in the real world is all. It's not all pretty and tied up in a bow for all of us."

"Everyone has pain and struggles in their lives."

We sat in awkward silence while Jay finished her coffee. I tried to make small talk, but she answered my open-ended questions with single-word answers. I wasn't sure how she managed to do that so successfully. With her coffee finished, she thanked me and headed out the door. I watched her get on a motorcycle and drive off into the dark.

I looked at the paper and locket. I asked for a piece of plastic wrap from the waitress and covered the locket so I didn't get any prints on it.

I'd only been home about 15 minutes when Drew arrived. I had enough time to change out of my clothes and be in pajamas on the couch when he walked through the door.

"Any new leads?"

"A couple of people had cocaine at Bill Andrews' party, and there were quite a few questionable females there."

"Really?"

"Really, but I'm not getting my hopes up. Bill Andrews is a jerk, and we all know it. But it appears to have been one of his guests who found his own escort and brought a few of her friends along. Bill claims to have had no knowledge, and the guest corroborated that story. We took him in for questioning."

"Did you arrest him?"

"No, but we had a come to Jesus meeting, you might say."

He grinned at me.

"About?"

"About the way he treats his wife and women in general, including the wives of others."

"I didn't tell -"

"Emmie did," he interrupted.

"I should've said something to Dana."

"Maybe so, but he had no right to yell at you and treat you the way he did. He was wrong. You'd better be getting an apology from him soon."

I reached into the pocket of my pajama pants.

"I have something for you. I tried to call you, but I couldn't get through."

I held out the plastic bag with the pendant.

"Jay texted, and I met her at a diner downtown. She said this belonged to Caroline, Amber. I really wish I knew what her real name

137

was. I didn't want to touch it and get prints on it or anything."

He shook his head at me.

"Why won't you listen to me?"

"I didn't do anything stupid. We were in a public place," I said as he looked at me with his eyes narrowed. He shook his head.

"It doesn't matter, Grace. Bad things happen in public places sometimes. Why doesn't she contact the police?"

"Because she says I'm the next best thing and that police don't like girls like her."

"I wish she'd come to us."

"I wish that, too, but she's afraid of going to jail. I can understand that. Drew, have you contacted Amber's mother?"

"We're still looking. A woman named Lucy in New Orleans. It's hard."

"What about an obituary from a few years ago of a kid with cancer?"

"We've checked that. Nothing has come up. She could have moved or lived somewhere else at the time. Who knows? Jay could've gotten the city wrong or Amber could've lied."

Drew sat on the edge of the couch and clasped his hands in front of him. He didn't look at me, but he stared at the floor. I felt helpless. I knew he was worried about not finding the killer and failing in his first homicide case.

I slid closer to him and took his hands.

"You'll find the killer, Drew. I have faith in you."

"It's like you said, Grace. We're running out of time," he said without looking up at me.

"Drew Ward, you're a better man than this. You'll find this killer. I know you will."

He glanced at me and gave a weak smile.

"Thanks for the info, babe. Maybe there are some prints on that locket."

13

Friday.

I didn't have a lot for Friday except to get ready for Claire's party on Saturday and a few corporate things, but Claire's event was enough in and of itself.

"So how was your spying last night?" Beth asked.

I looked at Emmie. I didn't tell Beth anything.

"I don't know what you're talking about."

"Oh please. I could see the gears turning in your head while we were dropping off flowers. I knew you were up to something. What is it they always say about the quiet ones? You've never fooled me, Grace Ward. I'm just mad you didn't ask me to come along."

I laughed.

"It wasn't exciting at all. Although I think I saw Jeff Patterson making a pass at Andi Schaffer," said Emmie.

"Those two are old news," said Beth. "And they think no one knows."

"Really? Jeff Patterson is my dentist. We've delivered flowers to their house for numerous dinner parties. I can't believe it," Emmie said as she shook her head.

"If you only knew," Beth added as she put her hand on her hip and looked at Emmie.

"Emmie's right. There was nothing exciting happening at that party. Beth, do you know something you aren't telling me?"

She tilted her head and raised an eyebrow.

"Whatever do you mean?" asked Beth giving us her best Scarlett O'Hara impression.

"You know; something useful."

"And the fact that Bill Andrews has a taste for high-class call girls wasn't useful?"

"It was in a way, but not in the way we were hoping. Now, I can't stand him even more. I didn't know that was possible. I need to know something about what Ken and Mrs. Langham said - gated communities. You've got lots of friends in gated communities. Is there anything going on in some of these houses that Drew should know about?"

"My friend, Mary Elizabeth, is still in town because her mother's been ill. She just went into hospice," she said.

I nodded. We'd created a lot of arrangements for her.

"Anyway, I called Mary Elizabeth yesterday to check on her. She said she didn't like the people who were renting out the house across the street. She thought there might be something going on."

"What did she say?"

"That these aren't the typical people who rent houses in the neighborhood during the tournament. Usually, the people are nice and polite. This year, there are some really expensive and flashy cars in the neighborhood, and lots of women with silicone and plastic, if you know what I mean. She said it looks more like a Hollywood premiere than your typical group of corporate golf fanatics."

"But it's Columbia County, isn't it?"

Beth nodded.

"I'll still tell Drew."

"Give him Mary Elizabeth's number too. She can fill him in."

"Thanks."

I called Drew right away and gave him the information.

With Emmie and Beth working on arrangements, I slipped into my office. I couldn't get my last dream off my mind. I'd had it again. That sense of being placed into the dark and not knowing where I was. I was with them. I was taken captive with them, and I had no way of getting in touch with Drew. Somehow though, I knew I was going to be fine. The weirdest thing of all was the man from the parking lot was now showing up in my dreams, and he was the one who told me everything was going to be fine. I knew he didn't kill Amber or whatever her name was, but I'd never seen him as my friend either. He showed up and told me he wouldn't let them hurt me. It was odd. I couldn't get this off my mind. I didn't tell Drew any of it. I just wrote down all of the details, and I knew that he would solve this. He probably didn't need my help any, but somehow I felt I would be in the middle of this when he did. The thought scared me a little, but at the same time, I wasn't afraid. I couldn't explain that to anyone because it sounded so ridiculous. Afraid but not afraid. I almost said something to Emmie, but as it turned out, I didn't have to. After a couple of hours, she knocked on my door and confronted me.

"Did you realize it's time to go home?"

I shook my head and looked at the clock. It was almost 6. I wondered where the time had gone.

"I'm sorry. I had no idea."

"Do you mind if I come in?"

"Sure, what's up?"

"I need to ask you that. Did you ever eat lunch today?"

"No, I didn't. I've been really busy. We've got several weddings coming up in May, and I had so many things to do. Did the flowers make it to the Jones' party tonight?"

"Yes, they did, and Dana Andrews' baby arrangement made it to her as well."

I nodded. Emmie gave me the look. I swear I'd seen Drew, my mother, and my first grade teacher give me that look. It usually meant they didn't believe me or were disappointed in something I did.

"You can save your 'busy' stuff for someone who doesn't work with you. You've been acting strange the past couple of days with all of this bravado. It's not like you at all. I know that you are worried about this murder case, but it's consuming you or something is. And it's not the baby situation either."

I tried to smile. She was right as usual.

"How do you always know when something is going on?"

"I'm your best friend."

"I think I've heard that one before."

Emmie gave me a cheerful smile as she sat down across from my desk. I didn't really think I could talk to her about the dreams I'd had. I couldn't look at her as I talked.

"But it wouldn't take your best friend to know that. Even Beth said something. Did you even hear her tell you she was leaving?"

"She talked to me?" I didn't hear her at all. I guess I had been consumed with my thoughts.

Emmie's eyes got big , and she shook her head at me.

"Come on, Grace. Let's go."

"Where?"

"Anywhere but here."

I shut down my computer.

"Let's go for a walk or to get a cup of coffee or a smoothie or something," she suggested.

"That sounds like an idea."

There was a coffee shop a block away. I needed some fresh air anyway. I didn't say much as we walked. I never drank their coffee because they had the best smoothies.

As we sat under the covered patio, Emmie didn't waste any time.

"Okay. Enough. What is going on with you?"

"It's these dreams. I've never had so many in such a short period of time. They mean something. I know they do. I've always prayed that my life would have purpose or meaning to help someone. Until now, I never felt I did anything important."

She stared at me.

"Of course, you've done important things."

I shook my head.

"Something bigger than me."

"Like?"

"I've had a few dreams that I don't know what to make of, Emmie."

"Well, you can tell me. You know you can tell me anything."

"Yes. I know I can, but I can't."

Emmie shook her head at me.

"I don't understand, hon."

"Neither do I."

I was having a hard time putting the words together. Sometimes what I felt didn't translate well into words.

"Just spit it out, sweetie."

I shrugged my shoulders as I stared into the frothy whipped cream covered strawberry smoothie. I played with the thick blue, plastic straw, swirling the pink liquid around. After a couple of minutes, I looked at her.

"Okay, the first part I can just spit out. The man I saw in the parking lot; the one I've seen outside the shop - I don't think he's dangerous."

Emmie scrunched her brow and narrowed her eyes at me.

"Really? How can you be sure?"

"I know this is going to sound stupid, but he showed up in a dream. He told me he wouldn't hurt me, and that everything was going to be okay. He also told me that he didn't kill Amber, but I already knew that. One part I don't understand though. He told me he was watching out for me so that I didn't get hurt."

Emmie just stared like she didn't believe me.

"Yep. That one I don't believe. So what else?"

"That's just it. I don't know. I can't explain what I'm feeling. These dreams. They've always been so vivid, so real, but recently they are more abstract and just plain weird. I've had some concrete things in them, but the rest is hazy. I wake up with something telling me that I'm going to help Drew solve this case. I don't think it's going to be in a way that he'd approve. It's like I know something is getting ready to happen, but I can't tell you why I know it or what it even is."

"You're losing me, Grace, and you're scaring me too."

"Don't be afraid. There's nothing to be afraid of. It's all going to be okay, but this may be the only way that I get through to Drew or these dreams get through to him."

"I don't get what you're saying."

"I know, and I'm sorry that I can't really explain it to you. My dreams are real."

"I know that."

"They've had real clues in them, but Drew still won't listen because he's mad about a couple of dreams I had that came true. We knew what was going to happen to Mark and Linda. I saw in the dream Drew trying to help them, but he would be too late. He's been angry at me every since - like it's my fault that it happened the way it did."

Emmie nodded.

"The latest dreams that I haven't even tried to share with Drew give me the impression that I'm going to be put in danger. Just so you know. I keep a dream journal. I write it all down. I keep it in the table next to the couch in the living room. Sometimes, it's on top; sometimes, I put it in the drawer."

"Why are you telling me this?"

"If I ever need you to get it for me, you should know where it is."

"I don't like the way this is sounding. Are you going somewhere?"

I reached out to touch Emmie's hand and smiled at her.

"I'm not scared so you shouldn't be either."

"Well, I'm glad you're all calm," she said.

She tilted her head to the right and stared at me.

"You really are calm, aren't you?"

"Yes, I'm going to help Drew solve this murder. He'll be the success he's always wanted to be."

"His success aside - are you sure you are going to be okay?"

I nodded.

"I know I will be, but there is danger on the way. I see myself in a warehouse or something like those girls are in, and I'm trapped. I hear a train whistle. That's all I remember."

"How's Drew been since he busted you?"

I laughed.

"He roared like a lion, but underneath he's a teddy bear. He told me he didn't want me to be in danger."

"And that's a very good husband thing to say."

"True."

"So what are your plans for tonight?"

"I need to make a flower arrangement for Dana Andrews from my mom and maybe from me too."

"Tonight?"

"My mother is going over there tomorrow, and I told her I'd make something for her to take with her."

"I can help if you want."

"I'm good. I haven't really challenged my creativity in a while, and I think I'd like to try that tonight. And everything Bill said was right even though it hurt. I should've done something instead of disappearing. Drew said he chatted with Bill the other night. I'm sure Bill didn't tell Dana. He would've had to admit that he was questioned by the police. I'm sure he's not going to tell her about his outside interests."

"Are you ready to see Dana?"

"Not yet."

"Look, if you need me, I'll be at home. I don't get the boys back until late Sunday night."

"Thanks, Emmie."

I walked back to the shop, and Emmie headed home. I stared at the flowers we had in the back. Nothing inspired me. I thought about Dana. I smiled. I wanted her to be happy, and I knew she was because she finally had what she always wanted. With a husband like Bill, she needed something good in her life. And Hope Lily Andrews was good for Dana. As odd as it sounded, the whole murder situation and trying to help Drew had gotten my mind off my own troubles. For a couple of days at least, I'd forgotten that pain.

When I got back to my work station, I noticed I had a few texts. One was from Drew telling me he'd be late. That wasn't a surprise. I think he'd work around the clock if it meant solving this case. He did say that he was having someone look into the party that Beth's friend had told him about. No stone unturned, I suppose. I also had one from Claire asking for an orchid arrangement for the wife of one of the businessmen in town for the tournament. She wanted it tonight before 9. The couple was scheduled in town later tonight. Fortunately for both of us, there were orchids in the arrangements she'd already ordered for Saturday's party, and I had some left.

After I finished those two, I dropped the first off at my mother's, and the second one, I had to drop off at a house not far from the one where Claire had her party.

I didn't stay long at my mother's.

"That's beautiful," she said as I brought it in.

"Thank you," I said as I gave her a hug.

"You don't want to stay for a little while? We just finished eating, but there's some left in the fridge in the butter containers. I just put the label stickers on there so you know what's what. There's some okra and tomatoes in one and green beans in another. Grilled chicken is in the biggest container."

"That sounds really good, but I have another arrangement I have to deliver tonight in a few minutes."

"Are you sure? You could take it with you."

"Maybe I'll come back."

"Okay. Let me know, and I love these flowers. I know Dana will too."

The next arrangement went to another big house. I wondered if I was late. She had said before 9 p.m. and it wasn't even 8. However there were tons of cars in front of the house. I went to the door and rang the bell.

A scantily clad woman came to the door. I thought I might've had the wrong house.

"I have a delivery? Oh, they're gorgeous," she exclaimed and took them from me. Then she slammed the door in my face. Somehow, I didn't think that was the wife.

There were long windows on either side of the door. I could see in, and she wasn't the only scantily clad woman in the room. I needed to call Drew. This looked much more suspicious than the party I'd crashed the night before.

When I got back into my car, I checked my phone because the address was in a text message. That was the house on the text, but if that was going on here, was there something Claire was hiding somewhere else? Bill had rented a couple of houses. I thought about the phone conversation I'd overheard. Who's to say Claire's group didn't have more than one location. Maybe the main party was a cover to throw the scent off? And that phone conversation referred to another party altogether. I wondered about Saturday's party. Was there more to it than met the eye? As I was trying to figure out what to do next, I got an obscure text from Jay.

She said she was afraid and wanted to meet me at my shop. I responded I could be there in 10 minutes.

Maybe now she'd talk to Drew? At least she'd talk to me. I wanted to help her. I knew she was in danger.

I tried calling Drew to let him know what was going on, but it went to his voicemail. I left him a message about the party I'd just left. Maybe I could call him when I met with Jay. I'd try calling him again later.

My shop was downtown, and it was good to see people out and about tonight after the day's play at the course. The restaurants seemed busy. I walked into my shop and turned on the lights while I waited for Jay. I sent her a text to let her know I'd arrived. It took me longer than I thought it would. I couldn't find a place to park. Usually, it wasn't a problem. I could park out behind the shop, but I didn't think I'd be here long. At least, I hoped not. I needed a fresh start in the morning.

I waited, but Jay didn't respond to my text.

Ten minutes passed; then a half an hour. I tried calling Drew, but he didn't answer either. I decided to leave another message.

"Hey, I guess you're having a busier night than you thought. Please give me a call."

Within a couple of minutes, Drew called me back.

"Where are you?"

"I'm at my shop. Jay is supposed to meet me here. She sent me a text saying she was scared. I'm scared for her. It's been almost two hours, Drew."

"Don't go anywhere. I'm on my way."

14

My husband's voice was the last thing I remembered until I came to with a splitting headache. I could see the moon slipping through the slats in the window. It looked like it was boarded up. I sat up. I was on a slab of cold, dusty concrete. I could feel the grit on my hands. I had no idea where I was or how I'd gotten there. I sat there for a few minutes while my eyes tried to adjust to the dim moonlight. My first thought was Drew. All that self-defense training he'd put me through over the years, and I'd forgotten to pay attention to my surroundings. Someone came in without my knowing because I hadn't gotten that stupid bell fixed. My gun was in my purse. A lot of good that did me. I felt the back of my head. Ouch. It was tender. I didn't remember getting hit, and I felt something in my neck. Like a needle? I was drugged? I shook my head. I did feel a little woozy. I tried to stand up. My legs felt unsure like a toddler wearing her mother's high heels. And then it hit me. I was in the middle of that dream I'd had except that this time it wasn't a dream. This was definitely real.

There had to be a door - an exit.

"I was wondering when you were gonna wake up," I heard a female voice behind me as I tried to steady myself on my feet. I almost lost my balance, but she came up behind me.

"You've been out for a good two hours," she said in a distinct Cajun twang. "I wondered if you were dead, but I could hear you breathing."

I couldn't really what she looked like. It was too dark. She was shorter than I was, but that's all I could tell.

"The name is Jazzy. It's a nickname from my younger days in New Orleans."

"Hi Jazzy. I'm Grace."

"And there's no way out," she said. She was cheerful despite being in this horrible place; wherever this place was.

"I'm confused."

"I know you are, sugar. You're not one of us."

"One of who? Are there others here? Where are we anyway, and how did I get here?"

I began to realize my head wasn't the only thing that hurt. My right shoulder and the right side of my hip hurt too. I think I was lying on my right side when I woke up. Was I thrown on the floor? I reached my left hand up to rub my shoulder. Just then I heard a train whistle, and the building began to move. I wondered how close we were to the tracks. My dream flashed across my mind. I wondered where Jay was. She never texted me, and who was Jazzy?

"You sure do ask a lot of questions. I don't really know where we are. I live in Atlanta. I was trying to get home where I could sing jazz and the blues, but I've never made it that far. They forced me to come to Augusta for this stupid golf tournament. They said I could make some good money with this and maybe they'd finally let me go. Everything was going great until this freaky rich man wanted me to..." she paused. "Well, there's stuff I don't do, and he roughed me up, split my lip and I have a swollen eye, and my cheek is bruised."

She started cursing under her breath.

"They threw me in this hole until it's all over."

I realized what she meant that I wasn't one of them. Of course, I had no way to get in touch with Drew - not that I could tell him where I was anyway. I didn't even know. When he said he was on the way, I wondered where he had to drive from to get to my shop? What did he think when he came in and couldn't find me? I guess my cell phone, purse, and gun were all still where I'd left them. I could hear his voice in my head telling me to get that bell fixed and asking me why I didn't listen to him. If I ever saw him again, I knew that would be the first thing he'd say.

"Do you know someone named Jay?"

"Nope, don't know nobody by that name."

I didn't say anything else. I just walked around the warehouse and heard a squeaking sound. A chill went down my spine. Was that a rat? I shuddered. There seemed to be a lot of crates around. I knew there were some warehouses downtown. Was that where we were? And who put me here? I had more questions than answers.

"Who put you here?"

"You look like a nice lady. I don't know what you're doing here. You ain't got no business in this place."

"Who brought me here? I don't know how I got here."

"I'm here because I messed up. I can't earn them any money with a broken up face like I've got right now. This was supposed to be a big week for them. I can't even cover this with makeup."

I wondered why she wouldn't answer my question. Was she one of the people who kidnapped me? Was she my babysitter now?

"Are you okay?"

I wished I could see her face better.

"It ain't nothing."

"I wish I could help you."

"Help me? I don't need anyone to help me. Besides, ain't nobody ever wanted to help me unless they could help themselves to me first."

"I'm sorry."

"I'm sure you are a nice person, but people like you don't help people like me."

She sounded exactly like Jay. Did other people think this way? Was that the reason they didn't take people's help when it was offered? Who were people like me?

"So have you tried to get out of here?"

"It's easier to see in the day light, but there's aren't too many windows here. It's a warehouse. There's one or two windows in the front of the building, and they're boarded up. The door is bolted. There's a couple of vents or something up high."

"Do they always treat you like this?"

"It's not a life of comfort. You don't bring home the money then you get punished for it. I've been trying to save up, but who am I trying to fool? You don't do what the men want, and you get beat up. Then, you can't bring home any money til you heal up. There's another tournament next week that they'll take us to, but I won't be able to make money then either. Not a lot of stuff over the summer. I heard some of the girls are going to be shipped overseas. I might be one of them if I heal. I hope I never heal. Then, I'll really never make it back to New Orleans."

I sat back down on the floor.

"How long have you been in here?"

"Since yesterday. They'll keep me here until Monday when we all go home. And then I don't know. It's not the first time this has happened."

"Do you think it will be Monday before they come back?"

"I don't know. It's Friday right? Maybe Saturday. Maybe Sunday."

This had been the longest couple of weeks of my life. It seemed like an eternity ago that Amber had died, and here I was now not able to reach my husband and wondering who'd taken me and what they wanted.

"How'd you end up with these people, Jazzy?"

"You sure are talkative."

I laughed.

"So are you."

She laughed too.

"My grand mama said I could talk to walls. I didn't need anyone to answer me, and the walls weren't going anywhere."

I laughed.

"I lived in New Orleans until I was 10. When Katrina hit, we lost everything. My grand mama died. She refused to evacuate. She wouldn't listen to my mama and me. We begged her."

Jazzy's tone dropped. Before it was lilting and sassy; now it was low and devoid of all the joy. She paused.

"We stayed at the dome, but it was too crowded. It smelled bad, and there were so many people. We accidentally got separated and put on different buses - my three brothers, Mama, and me. I was scared. Somehow I made it to relatives outside Atlanta. Mama and my brothers made it there too. She tried to make it. When my grand mama died, Mama fell apart. She got addicted to drugs. She always said - 'Jazzy, you can make something of yourself. Make your mama proud.'"

I tried to look at her through the thin shaft of moonlight.

"I was 12 when Mama died. My aunt was on social security. She couldn't take care of four kids. She tried, but she couldn't. Then, she had a stroke. They took us into foster care. I couldn't stay there. I was separated from my brothers. Nobody is going to take four kids. My mama and grand mama were gone. My aunt was gone. By the time I was 14, I ran away. I thought if I made it back to New Orleans, I could be happy again, but I couldn't make it to New Orleans. These men promised to help me get there if I helped them. If you know what I'm saying.'

"I do," I whispered.

"I just want to make my mama and grand mama proud." I could hear the tears in her voice. "My grand mama took lots of odd jobs in her life. She worked in some beautiful houses in New Orleans. She'd take me there sometimes. I always wanted to decorate houses."

"Okay. So we need to get out of here."

"Good luck with that. Even if we did, there are men with guns out there ready to shoot us."

"You think?"

"Well, I've seen it before."

"Really? When?"

"A couple of years ago. They'd taken me to some big football game in Miami. It was just one night, but one of the girls didn't come back with us. Some said she ran away, but the rest of us knew better. The rest of us knew she was dead."

"They've killed girls?"

"Okay, I've never actually seen them do it - like point the gun at them and shoot them, but you just know things."

"Did you know a blonde named Amber?"

"Yeah, we knew Amber. She was a good kid. She wanted to go home. She was from Louisiana too. She lived in Alexandria. She wanted to leave this life. She tried to get us to go with her, but they -
"

Jazzy paused and shook her head.

"What did they do?"

"They tattooed her up for some rich guy in some crazy country I've never heard of. He only wants blondes. He likes them best with green eyes, but blue will do. He wanted a butterfly tattoo on her arm to show she belonged to him. It was like a brand. There are other girls with that tattoo. It shows they are his property."

Jay had a small one, but Jay wasn't blonde. I guess she could've been blonde at some point.

"Who is he?"

"I can't tell you. I've told you too much."

"Jazzy, I want to help you."

"I can't talk about it. I don't want to go to him. I know that what they tell everyone about him isn't true. They tell them that he lives in this palace in the jungle somewhere in South America, and they live a great life. But I don't believe it. Something just tells me it's not right. I can hear my grand mama telling me to stay away. I know that's stupid because she's dead. My grand mama was right about a lot of things. I don't know why she didn't leave Katrina. I need her."

"Jazzy, how many other girls are we talking about?"

"Well, it's not like we all live together or anything. There's a lot, but they do send a lot of them away. If they send that many away, I don't want to know what he does to them."

"Do they all get tattoos?"

"Only the ones he buys."

I guess that would explain why they tried to remove the tattoo and the reason no one would put it on social media, as beautiful as it was.

"Why can't you get away?"

"It's not that easy. They know how to find us. A few of us live together. They know how much we bring in. They know if we skim any off the top. They're like Santa except without the presents. They know when you go to sleep, when you wake up. They know everything."

"How?"

Jazzy grabbed my hand and slid my finger over her wrist. I felt something like a nodule. I wasn't really sure what it was.

"It's a chip - like you put in a dog or a cat."

It might have been a warm Georgia spring night, but I could feel the hairs standing up on my arms and a chill go down my spine as her words sunk into me. Jazzy really was a modern day slave.

We sat on the floor for several more minutes. I could only imagine what had happened to Jay. Maybe they kidnapped me because of her. Maybe she was locked up in another warehouse in this set of buildings. I didn't know what they wanted with me. Was it to keep me out of the way? Was Claire's Saturday party the one we'd been searching for? Was Jay the key or was Jazzy? I had to get to Drew. Drew. That was it. It wasn't about me at all. It was about getting to Drew and getting his attention off this case and on trying to find me. But who knew what he was investigating? Ken and Janice knew that he was on the case. I know Jay tried to make it seem like Ken and Janice were up to no good, but they seemed so nice. Claire couldn't have possibly known about Drew, could she? I didn't ever tell her anything about my husband, unless she saw us outside the party. Drew knew we were there and so did Beth. Maybe we hadn't been as cautious or sneaky as we'd thought. And then there was the mysterious man who kept showing up. I was still alive so I figured the odds were in my favor, and I really didn't think they wanted to kill me. I wondered if I'd seen one too many spy movies at this point.

"Jazzy, we're going to get out of here," I said as I stood back up.

"There's no way out until they come back to get us."

"Well, I'm not going to wait around until they do. If we've got time, I'm going to use it."

I couldn't take - no - for an answer. I had to get Jazzy out, and I had to get me out. I had to talk to my husband, and now I had a witness I could take back to Drew. Jazzy could be the key to solving the whole mystery. The light was coming through the top of the building, and the warehouse was at least two floors. I kept thinking back to my dreams. I'd seen women in places like this. I wondered if there were other buildings and if the other girls were being kept here. Surely, they didn't just pack them into crates, put them on trains, and ship them like a bunch of cargo.

"Jazzy, tell me what this place looks like in the day time."

"You think we're really going to get out? Lady, you're crazy."

"Like you said, I'm not one of you. They wouldn't get top dollar for me. That's not the reason they took me. They've put me here to keep me out of the way because I'm interfering with their plans. And I don't want to think about what will happen to me when they don't need me anymore."

"Who are you, lady?"

"That's a good question."

Jazzy stood up too.

"Well, I like crazy people," she said. Her tone had perked back up. That was a good sign.

I walked around the warehouse. There were wooden pallets and some crates. I found the door and shook it. I could hear the jangle of chains. Jazzy was right. That was not a way out. The moment I did that I felt fear try to grip me. What if someone was outside? I shrank back and held my breath. After what seemed like forever, there was no noise from the outside. My heart felt like it was in my throat as I slowly exhaled. We were alone.

"What happens if we get out of here?" Jazzy asked.

"I'm going to take you someplace safe."

"There's no place like that for me."

"We'll find a place."

I looked around. I had on low heels, but they weren't exactly the type of shoes I needed to climb on things. I wondered how heavy the pallets and crates were. Maybe we could stack them up to form a ladder, but I didn't know if we could get it high enough that I could actually reach the top. I wasn't exactly tall, and Jazzy was shorter than I was.

"Let's push some of these crates together and see how close we can get us to that vent up there."

The crates scraped across the bottom of the floor. We tried to form stairs with the crates, stacking them against the wall in the shape of a triangle. There were several sturdy boxes and pallets in the warehouse, but not enough for a complex stairway to the top the warehouse. I didn't relish the idea of standing on top of a wobbly tower although if it meant getting out of this place, I might've been willing to try it. There were some metal frames in the expansive room, but they were bolted to the cement.

I stood at the bottom of our makeshift staircase and stared.

"The last boxes are against that wall. It's not enough," said Jazzy.

"No, it's not enough."

I walked through the warehouse and tried to gather my thoughts. My shoulders hurt; my head hurt; I was tired and hungry. I couldn't get out of this place, and I had no idea what they were going to do to me when they came back - whoever they were. I wondered what happened to Jay. Were the people who kidnapped me the same ones who had Jay?

From the dim light, I could tell there were a few more crates. Not enough just like Jazzy said. I stood back and turned toward the stairs we'd made. I could see its silhouette. As I pondered everything, I leaned back against the wall. It wasn't flat. I turned back around and slid my hand along the wall. It felt like a door.

"Jazzy, I think I found something."

I tried to push the crates away, but I couldn't. They were heavy as though they still contained their discarded and forgotten cargo.

"Like what?"

"Let's try to move the boxes out of the way. It feels like a door behind this."

"It's probably just another locked door."

"Well, I've got to try."

Using our weight, we managed to push the crates slightly; at least, it was enough to get to the door, and to my surprise, it wasn't locked. The door opened into another warehouse. However, this warehouse had windows along one side, and these windows weren't boarded over. I walked over to the roll-up bay doors. I pushed and pulled, but they were locked. From the rich orange flooding the room, I could tell the sun was rising outside. We walked into the room, and I noticed makeshift rooms. They were divided with flimsy material, simple cubicles with cots inside them. They were empty now, but it was obvious that they'd been inhabited recently. Did they bring the girls here first? What was this place? It didn't look like the type of set up a bunch of homeless people had erected. There were odd things like mirrors and makeup pallets - lipsticks, eye shadows with a rainbow of colors. And lots and lots of needles.

I turned around to get a glimpse at Jazzy. Her face was bloodied, and her right eye was so swollen I wasn't sure how she could even see out of it. Her lip was mangled as well. I walked over to her.

"We need someone to look at that for you."

She shook her head.

"I'll be okay. Always am."

"Do you recognize this place?"

She shook her head.

"I was in a really nice house, but I heard talk that there were other girls in other places like this."

It was Saturday - the day of another big party. I guess Emmie and Beth would carry on without me. Claire had paid a deposit, but after tonight, she'd pay the balance. What was I thinking? I was worried about money at a time like this? How could I possibly be thinking about that? My thoughts were all over the place. They jumped from my business to getting out of here alive to my husband. I wondered what Drew was doing. I'm sure he was looking for me. He said he was on his way to my shop. I wondered if my mother knew. I wondered about Emmie and Beth. They had keys. I hoped they'd open the shop and take care of everything.

As I walked along looking in these makeshift rooms, I heard a train whistle. The floor began to rattle. My dreams came flooding back to me. Some of this was beginning to make sense. And if it was daylight, someone would be down here looking for us soon.

"Jazzy, we've got to find a way out of here. Maybe there's another door."

It was at time like this when I wished I'd gone with Drew and his friends when they went rock climbing. I had a great imagination. In some movie, the heroine in this situation would grab a rope and lasso it around the top of the rolling door and climb up it to the top where she'd look out the windows. Then, she'd use her legs to springboard her backwards and gain momentum to break through the glass and rappel down the other side. But I knew I couldn't do that.

"How athletic are you?"

I asked that and laughed. Somehow I didn't see Jazzy as a female super hero either.

"What about those boxes we've been dragging around all night? Those windows are a whole lot lower in here than the ones in here."

"Jazzy, you're a genius, and I'm really tired."

The scraping sound of the boxes as we dragged them across the floor must've drowned out the sound of the door being opened in the other warehouse.

"My, aren't we resourceful?" rang out the female voice.

I'd heard that voice before. I recognized it right away. I turned around.

"Jay?"

She didn't look like Jay. She had gorgeous long blonde hair and was dressed in a high-powered suit with fabulous stiletto heels. Her face had no signs of the marks I saw the other night. And she certainly wasn't afraid. Instead, I only saw anger.

"Actually, it's Jillian," she sneered as she walked toward me. She only had one bodyguard with her. Maybe the fact that I looked totally unable to defend myself could work for me.

She kept walking until she was centimeters from my face. Her heels made her slightly taller than me. Her cold blue eyes stared into mine, but I wasn't about to flinch for her.

"Your husband was supposed to come to your and my rescue last night at your shop. I know that you texted him that you were meeting me. Instead, he ended up costing me a lot of money. I knew I had to get revenge when he crashed the wrong party and arrested too many of my girls."

"Good for him."

A stinging slap came from out of nowhere across my cheek.

"And to think, I almost liked you. He cost me a lot of money, Mrs. Ward, I mean a lot of money," her eyes glinted as her tone dropped to a menacing low. "Those girls are supposed to be on route to Dubai after this weekend, but my buyer got cold feet because of the bust and has called off this deal and possibly future ones..."

She paused and stared at me.

"We could dye your hair blonde."

"I'm not a piece of merchandise," I snapped back.

"You're too old anyway. You're tainted," she said.

She snapped her fingers, and the bodyguard lurched forward. I hadn't noticed it until now, but he was the man from the parking lot, the man with Amber.

"So you recognize Frank?"

I must've reacted to him.

She cocked her head to the side and sneered at me.

"Of course you do. You told me about seeing him with Amber.

160

Sadly, he wasn't the one who killed Amber. I did. She was going to walk away from a multi-million dollar deal. At least, it would've been for me because this was to be the first of many deals. She was going to take precious assets with her. She'd convinced several other girls to join up with those church freaks. I'd kill you myself, but I don't have time for it. And I can't get blood on these amazing shoes. I have to look my best when I patch up this deal with a wealthy sheik and make a second deal when I get the ladies out of jail."

I watched as Frank pulled a gun. Jillian smiled at me before turning to glance at Frank.

"I have a lot to do. Frank, I'll be back to pick you up later. Call me when you're done."

With that, she turned and walked out of the warehouse. I stared at Frank, not sure of what was going to happen next. He didn't say anything. None of the self-defense techniques that Drew had taught me were coming to mind immediately, but then muscle memory or the last of my adrenaline kicked in. I wasn't going to die without a fight. I charged at him with the intent of kneeing him in the groin, but somehow I ended up with my back pressed against his chest and his hand over my mouth. I struggled. I think I tried to bite him, but then he whispered in my ear.

"Mrs. Ward, that was a good move, but I'm with the FBI."

My arms became limp, and I stopped struggling. I was out of breath and I felt numb as I tried to make sense of so many things speeding through my brain at one time. This was the man I'd seen with Amber. He released me, and I turned around to stare at him. He'd put his gun away at some point.

"But I saw you with Amber."

"I know. I can explain everything, but I think there's someone you need to see first."

He turned and gestured for me to walk in front of him. As I walked back into the first warehouse, I saw Drew. He raced toward me. I'd never been so happy to see someone in my life. There were tears in his eyes as he embraced me. He squeezed me so tightly that

I wasn't sure I could breathe, and then the emotions hit me. My adrenaline was completely gone, and the fear that I'd never see him again rushed to the surface. The sobs seemed to overtake me for several minutes as I rested my head against his chest.

"It's okay, babe. It's okay," he whispered, holding me close to him. I felt safe.

"I'm sorry I didn't get the door bell at the shop fixed," I said when I could finally get something out.

"I have someone there now," he whispered.

"This early?"

I started laughing through the tears. I was a mess. He let me go, and I looked at him.

"You said you were on the way last night."

"I was. Come sit down for a minute."

Drew took my hand and led me to one of the crates in my makeshift staircase.

"This is Special Agent Frank Monroe with the FBI."

"Call me Frank. I'm sorry about all you've gone through, and I apologize for scaring you. I wanted to be able to talk to you and put you at ease, but I couldn't blow my cover," Frank said.

"I don't understand."

"I've been part of Jillian's operation for a while, but I never felt she trusted me completely. We wanted to get all of her operation, not just a piece, and we were so close. Her organization is only a tiny part of a huge conglomerate. The bust last night forced her to take some action she wasn't ready to take, but we've got her now."

He shook his head.

"Jillian and I were there when you found Amber's body. Jillian's a control freak, and she heard it over the police scanner. She dressed as Jay, and I dressed as a homeless guy. She saw you and your husband at the river. The girl you found wasn't named Amber, and she wasn't Caroline or whatever you were told. Jillian wanted you and your husband to chase another rabbit trail."

I nodded.

"Her name was Christy. Amber was the code word for Jillian's operation because there was oil money tied up in it. Christy had been groomed for meeting this sheik. She was sweet and innocent looking, something this particular buyer wanted and had a market for. Like I said, Jillian never completely trusted me; she watched me like a hawk. On the night you saw me with Christy, I had just told Christy that she was going to have to go to Dubai even though I knew she didn't want to go. She didn't have a choice. She was angry and scared, and I don't blame her. I tried to tell her it wasn't what she thought, but I couldn't tell her I was with the FBI just yet."

He shook his head.

"That night, Jillian came down from Atlanta. We were here for some advance scouting of the city. Jillian gave me something to drink, and there was something in it that knocked me out. I think Jillian suspected I wanted to help Christy. She got me out of the way so she could be with Christy. I have a feeling Christy told her she wasn't going to Dubai. She'd met Ken and Janice and planned to get out of Jillian's organization. Plus, she'd talked other girls into leaving with her. She thought Jillian wouldn't stop her if a bunch of them left at one time. That would have cost Jillian a ton of money just like she said. In a rage, Jillian killed Christy. Jillian has never learned to control her temper. I think she did it to keep the other girls in line. There were about 100 girls in Atlanta she planned to send overseas, and there were a few she'd brought here to meet with the sheik. The parties were places they could see the goods before signing the final contract so to speak. She had two new guys dump the body. I have a feeling you won't be finding their bodies any time soon, Drew. I was surprised she confessed it to you, Mrs. Ward, a little while ago, but at that point, it really didn't matter to her. And I have it all recorded."

He smiled and nodded at Drew.

"She called me last night from your cell phone, babe," Drew interjected. "She said she'd gotten to your shop and you were missing. By then, she'd gotten wind that we'd crashed her party, and in her anger, she kidnapped you. She said she'd heard something about a warehouse and girls. She told me she'd find out more and call me this morning. I didn't know that Jillian and Jay were the same person until Frank called around 2 this morning. We met in person about 30 minutes later, and he told me everything that was going on. He said he didn't know where she was holding you, but he promised me that he'd help me find you. Jillian's call this morning came in about 15 minutes ago. She told me where to come find you. She pretended to be afraid for your life. She told me about a man and a gun. I figured she had Frank with her."

"She walked away from me for a few minutes when we first arrived. I saw her with a phone that I knew wasn't hers. Her plan was have me caught red-handed killing a cop's wife or so she thought," said Frank. "At worst, she thought Drew could have gotten me on kidnapping, and there is a gun with my prints on it that was going to resurface soon as evidence I killed Christy. Her plan was to pin both murders on me. She wanted to pin everything on me; that's the reason she watched and recorded all my movements. That would have given her the time she needed to get out of town. I got word to Drew a few days ago. I had to tell the police what was going on so the local officials didn't blow our investigation. But the only times I saw your husband face to face was in the parking lot of that restaurant, where I'd taken Christy in hopes of calming her down, and earlier this morning."

He smiled.

"Like I said, we wanted to bring down the whole operation not just a piece. We needed a little more time and evidence. Last night, I got some key pieces, and this morning, I have everything I need. Now I can get her on first-degree murder charges. That alone should warrant the death penalty, plus there's kidnapping, human trafficking, and racketeering. And she tipped her hand with her bigger plans. I know her contacts and who she's worked through to arrange these deals. Who knows? She may even try to weasel her way out and give up her bosses. That's what we wanted. Another agent is working on that now. He'll have her in custody within the hour."

"I'll testify against that witch any day of the week."

I'd forgotten that Jazzy was in the warehouse.

"She's ruined my life long enough."

"Thank you, Jasmine," Frank said.

He looked at me.

"Just so you know, Mrs. Ward, your dream journal was accurate. And I'm glad I tried to let you know that everything was going to be okay even if it was only in the dream."

I was surprised when he said that. I turned to look at Drew.

"I found it and showed it to him. I needed to know," Drew said.

"You're obviously in one of the places now that you saw in your dream," Frank said.

Just then, another train whistle began to blow.

"I haven't always believed in that stuff," said Frank. "There are a lot of nut jobs that claim to be psychic."

"I'm not a psychic."

"That's the reason I took a look at it for Drew. I've seen a couple of people who had some uncanny knack for things that I couldn't explain. Mrs. Ward, I had no idea that Jillian would snap and kidnap you. I thought she was just using you to throw your husband off the scent. But in the past couple of months, she's gone off the deep end."

I turned to look at Drew. He squeezed my hand.

"Jillian had girls spread out all over town. She was super cautious. She didn't tell me where everyone was, and I didn't even know about this place," said Frank.

"I didn't sleep last night, babe. I'm so sorry you had to go through this."

I thought Drew was going to break down and cry.

"I wanted to be involved, Drew" I said. "Who knows I may look back on this experience as being a good one - one day."

I tried to laugh, but Drew shook his head at me.

"I will never let you go through anything like this again, Gracie. Never again."

I still had a few more questions.

"What about Bill Andrews?"

Frank didn't answer at first.

"He's not mixed up in this particular case."

I didn't like his response. That only meant that Bill was clean where this investigation was concerned. I thought about what Beth had said. I needed to visit Dana.

"Claire?"

Frank shook his head.

"No, she's totally innocent in all of this. And she sent you to the wrong house last night, but it turned out to be a key to this case."

I laughed. I was glad of that. I liked Claire.

"But the party Beth told you was the one we busted last night that made Jillian angry," said Drew.

"I think we owe Beth a dinner."

Drew laughed.

"You're probably right."

"What about the car and the man who died earlier this year?" I asked.

"That was another location where the girls stayed. The guy's nephew was in on this too," said Frank. "Like I said she was trying to pin a lot of things on me. Riding around in a car with stolen plates. She knew you had seen Amber and me, and she wanted to frighten you so she had me follow you. I know you saw me. I'm sorry for that too."

"So now what happens to the girls now?"

"It's a long and complicated process, I'm afraid," said Frank.

"Is there anything I can do?"

Frank smiled.

"Anything? You mean anything else, don't you? Mrs. Ward, you were a key to bringing this whole thing down."

"What happens to Jazzy?"

"Yeah, hey, what does happen to me? She controlled my life. I dreamed of a day when I wouldn't have to do what she wanted."

"Listen, Jazz, I have some people who need to talk to you, and

Mrs. Ward, I know there are people who want to talk to you as well," said Frank.

I hadn't noticed it, but there were a few other deputies as well as some people wearing FBI vests on the scene.

Drew and I were left alone for a few minutes while Frank took Jazzy to have someone look at her injuries.

"Are you okay?"

"I'm fine. I'm tired. My body hurts."

"We need to get you checked out," he said.

"I'm fine, Drew."

A wave of relief swept over me, and I could finally smile.

"What?" he asked.

"You solved your first murder case. That's something to celebrate."

He didn't respond to that remark. Instead he leaned over and kissed me. He stared at me for a few moments as tears pooled in his eyes. He started to speak, and his voice shook.

"Last night, I had a lot of time to think and pray since there was no way I was going to sleep. I thought you walking out on me a couple of days ago shook me up, but this, this sealed the deal for me. I've never been so scared in my life as when Frank told me that he didn't know where you were. I can't lose you, Grace Ward. I just can't. I never thought I'd make a bargain with God, but I did. You're all I need. And if that means we never have children together, I don't care. I married you for you not for children."

"Drew -"

"I know what you're going to say. It's about the drinking. My bargain with God was if we found you alive, I'd stop drinking. I want to, but I can't stop by myself. I keep thinking back to that day when Mark and Linda - " he paused and looked away. "The day they died. I knew he had a drinking problem. I knew it was destroying him and Linda. I couldn't get him to listen to me. I keep thinking I could've stopped what happened that day. Your dream did warn me. I just wanted it to turn out differently. I'm not ready to talk about

167

everything that happened that day with you. I may never be able to talk about it, but I promise our path won't end up like theirs. I'm not going to let that happen. Like I said, I had a long talk with the Man upstairs."

I leaned my head on his chest.

"He's not the only one I talked to. Did you know Pastor B answers his phone at all hours of the night?"

I lifted my head and looked at him.

"His wife does too. I've had to call her before at 3 a.m.," I said and laughed.

"He's going to help me get help. I know I can't do this alone. And if you aren't here none of it matters anyway. I want us to get through this together. It may take some time."

"I promised you forever, Drew. You can have all the time you need."

He touched my cheek.

"Thank you, Grace, for helping me solve my first murder case."

"I told you it wouldn't end up as a cold case."

"That you did."

"And you know where to find me next time."

I smiled and winked at him.

"Who said anything about a next time, Mrs. Detective?"

"Just putting it out there."

Reach Charmain Z. Brackett on Facebook at www. facebook.com/thekeyofelyon or sign up for her newsletter at www. charmainzbrackett.com. Read her other titles, such as her Victoria James' mystery series, at www.amazon.com.